GERRY ANDERSON'S

GEMINI ● FORCE
1

BLACK HORIZON
M. G. HARRIS

Orion
Children's Books

First published in Great Britain in 2014 by Gollancz
This edition first published in 2015
by Orion Children's Books
An imprint of the Orion Publishing Group
Orion House
5 Upper St Martin's Lane
London WC2H 9EA
An Hachette UK company

The Orion Publishing Group's policy is to use papers that are natural,
renewable and recyclable products and made from wood grown
in sustainable forests. The logging and manufacturing processes are
expected to conform to the environmental regulations of the
country of origin.

A CIP catalogue record for this book is available
from the British Library

ISBN 978 1 4440 1406 8

Typeset at The Spartan Press Ltd,
Lymington, Hants

Printed and bound at CPI Group (UK) Ltd,
Croydon CR0 4YY

www.orionbooks.co.uk

For GERRY ANDERSON

*Thanks for so many wonderful years of entertainment,
for your brilliant mind and inspiration.
You'll always be remembered.*

How *Gerry Anderson's Gemini Force One* Got off the Ground

An introduction from
Gerry's younger son Jamie

After completing work on what would be his final television series (*New Captain Scarlet*) my father – Gerry Anderson (creator of cult classics like *Fireball XL5, Thunderbirds* and *Space: 1999*) – began work on a new sci-fi adventure series. However, this time it wasn't a TV series or a film … it was a novel.

As he worked I could see something really thrilling emerging. Something with all the excitement and adventure you might expect from an episode of his most famous creation – *Thunderbirds* – combined with a more modern feel that he'd started to explore in his *New Captain Scarlet* series.

Sadly, it soon became apparent to us – and to him – that he was already living with Alzheimer's disease. And so, over time, his progress on the book slowed.

Eventually he was forced to stop work as his ability to read and write was taken from him. It seemed so cruel that a man who loved nothing more than to write and create was no longer able to do so. Even so – his desire to get this final project rolling stuck with him right up until the end.

Dad died on 26th December 2012.

In the days and weeks after Dad's funeral, I began to piece together the projects he'd been working on before he was forced to abandon them due to his dementia. I really felt there was something special in this final project, and started to explore the possibility of getting it completed.

Not too long after I'd started working on it, I met with M.G. Harris. She wrote a treatment of the first few chapters using material Dad had left behind. When I read it, things suddenly felt like they'd fallen into place. The content, the dialogue, the pace ... it all felt so authentic. We had our author! We also finally decided on a name for the project – Gemini Force One.

We approached a number of publishers, but we couldn't seem to find one who would take the project without changing so many elements of the story that it no longer felt like a Gerry Anderson creation. So we turned to the crowdfunding website, Kickstarter.

After a month of planning, we launched the campaign. The response blew us away. Over 600 fans from all over the world put their own hard-earned cash into our project to make sure we could complete and publish the book in the way that Dad would have wanted.

And the good news didn't stop there – a short time later, we had a very exciting meeting with Orion. They loved the book and, best of all, they didn't want to change it! Very soon, we'd struck a deal to publish Gemini Force One!

I'm amazed that so much has happened in such a short time, and that we're now in a position to introduce Gemini Force One to new and existing Gerry Anderson fans all over the world. I'm incredibly grateful to those who have helped us make this happen – all of our wonderful Kickstarter backers, M.G. Harris, our agent Robert Kirby, and of course Amber and the team at Orion.

Stand by for action!

⟶ SKY-HIGH ⟵

The air was very clear that day, unusually free of the dry sand that often swept up from the surrounding desert.

Ben Carrington turned to catch a covert glimpse of the press photographers. They were packed in tight behind the velvet rope, straining for a good shot of his mother. In the blinding sunlight you couldn't tell, but behind her owl-like black sunglasses, Countess Caroline Brandis-Carrington was pale with anxiety.

Tragic widow gazes at her dead husband's final work.

That's the story the press would be looking for.

Ben lowered his camcorder. He placed a protective hand on his mother's shoulder. It was what his father would have done. Now it was Ben's turn. After all, he was sixteen years old; old enough to join the army and marry. Certainly old enough to be the one to comfort Caroline.

Every few seconds his mother's stare moved nervously along the sleek, vertiginous contours of the Carrington Sky-High Hotel. Ben was reluctant to follow her gaze. Maybe it was the blinding light of the sun. Or maybe it was the memory of watching someone fall.

It shouldn't be like this. Dad should be here, Ben thought.

The Sky-High had been Casper Carrington's grandest

project. It measured three hundred and two metres in height. It towered almost one hundred metres above the next highest building in Abu Dhabi. Globally, it was in the top ten.

Last week in the Himalayas, Ben's father had fallen a mere third of the hotel's height, but it had been enough to compress his torso and legs into the same space.

Instant death.

Caroline hadn't wanted Ben to see his father's body, but Ben had insisted. 'I'm not letting you do this alone.'

Now, under the Sky-High, Ben watched a sad smile touch his mother's lips. 'It had to be this one,' she murmured. 'As if we haven't all had enough of heights.'

Ben knew exactly what she meant and, after what had happened to his father, he'd understand if she didn't want him to climb, ever again. But every true climber knew at least one person who'd fallen to their death. No exceptions.

'The air display should be starting any minute,' was all he said. 'Try to look suitably dazzled. It was Dad's idea, after all.'

He had to shout the last few words. Three Aermacchi MB-339As roared across the sky. They trailed smoke in blue, yellow and black: the corporate colours of Carrington International. The colours foamed, lurid against the pale, clear sky of the desert.

A bemused voice behind them cut in. 'The air display was Carrington's idea? How very flamboyant of him!'

Ben tore his attention away from the sky for a

moment. He glanced at the man who'd addressed them: tall, slim but not slight, with a thick head of silver-grey hair and a rugged face that Ben supposed was pretty handsome for an older guy. There was something terribly familiar about him.

He stuck out a hand. 'Hi. I'm Benedict Carrington.'

The silver-haired man returned his handshake. 'Good to know you, Benedict. I knew your father, slightly. This air display ...' he glanced up, '... inspiring stuff. And brave of you to continue, in the circumstances.'

Caroline turned to the man. 'And you are?' she said, rather abruptly.

'Sorry, ma'am.' He gave a charming smile and offered his hand. 'My name's Jason Truby. And I didn't mean to suggest anything untoward. Truth is, I'm filled with admiration. It must have taken a lot of guts to show up today.'

Caroline seemed a little flustered. To Ben's surprise, instead of refuting his suggestion she said, 'Yes. Yes, I'm afraid it did.'

Ben continued to stare at the newcomer. That face. He knew it. Where from? Then it hit him. 'You're Jason Truby! From Trubycom! He went to *space*, Mum. Actual space!'

The display team made another pass, louder this time. They drew three intersecting lines with their smoke as they narrowly missed each other, a hundred metres above the pinnacle of the Sky-High.

Caroline inclined her head, briefly. 'You're an astronaut?'

'Yeah – the Gemini Mission!' Ben was awed. 'Trubycom funded it, didn't they? You landed on that asteroid, *1036 Ganymed*.'

'It was a while ago,' Truby said, modestly. 'And I'm no astronaut, that's for sure. Just between us, I was kind of feeble up there. Those guys from NASA took good care of me, but thanks for remembering, son.'

'I read loads of interviews with you,' Ben continued, 'when I was a kid.'

'How did you know my husband?' Caroline asked. She lifted her gaze once again towards the contrails in the sky.

'I tripped the right level on the rewards system. At Black Diamond, you get to meet the boss himself.'

'You're Black Diamond?' Ben said. 'Wow! There's only, like, a dozen of those.'

'All I can tell you is that your old man knew how to fix one heck of a good Manhattan.'

'That's right.' Caroline's attention swung back to Truby. 'He did. I taught him.'

Truby murmured, 'Lucky ol' Carrington.'

'It was a fair trade. He taught me a lot, too.'

But there was nothing he could teach you about climbing, Ben reflected. If only his father could have acknowledged that Caroline, with her alpine childhood and brief mountain-rescue career, was, by a considerable distance, his superior when it came to mountaineering.

Then he might have listened to her last week in the Himalayas. He'd almost certainly still be alive.

'So tell me, Mr Jason Truby. What is a telecoms tycoon and part-time astronaut doing at the opening of my husband's finest hotel?'

Truby put both hands in the pockets of his light-grey suit. He shrugged. 'Well, Mrs Carrington ...'

'It's *Countess*, actually. Since we're being formal.' The faint traces of his mother's Austrian accent were emphasised, Ben noted.

'Oh, I wasn't aware that Carrington was a count.'

Humourlessly, his mother smiled. 'He wasn't. But my father was.'

'Countess, then, and I hope you'll forgive this old Yank for a *faux pas*. I just happened to be in town for the superconductor conference. Thought I'd come along for the spectacle. It's terrible, what happened to Carrington. My sincere condolences.'

The air was once again shattered as the three Aermacchi screamed into formation above them.

'How pretty,' Caroline commented. 'They're forming a heart.'

Truby, however, visibly tensed, like a man hearing a burglar in his house. 'The blue pilot seems a little off.'

There was a deeper rumble, the throaty rumble of a passenger jet. Ben swivelled around, looking for the source of the sound. In the western corner of the sky he spotted it: a huge aeroplane – possibly an Airbus

A380 – was tilting into a descending turn about three kilometres away. He watched as it adjusted its trajectory.

'That plane ...' Ben muttered.

'It's going into a holding pattern,' Truby said. 'The airport must be busy.'

Ben watched, a cold dread slowly building inside his chest. 'But it's passing right over the air-display team.'

'The passengers will have a wonderful view,' Caroline remarked. She seemed distant again, disengaged. Ben glanced from her to Truby. Truby looked deadly serious now. He barely moved.

'Mum ... that plane's big enough to interfere with the air currents.'

'Darling, it's nowhere near them.'

'Benedict's right,' Truby said. 'The manoeuvres those pilots are doing – there's no room for error. Even the slightest alteration in the air currents can throw them off.'

'So why did the air-traffic controller let the other plane get this close?' Caroline asked.

'I don't know,' admitted Truby. 'Let's just hope they know what they're doing.'

Ben hunted for the three pilots in the sky. They'd split and were turning vertical loops at one-hundred-and-twenty-degree angles from each other. He felt his breath catch like a lump in his throat. Truby was right. The blue pilot was about a second behind the rest.

ROPE

In a crowd, fear travels faster than any other emotion. Truby was the first to point out that something was wrong but, seconds later, the murmurs started.

You could taste the anxiety in the air. All eyes were on the sky. Then the stray Aermacchi was flying off at a tangent, its right engine trailing black smoke. The pilot was bailing. He fell flat, plummeted like a plank, dragging a tangle of blue parachute silk.

A voice called out, 'His parachute hasn't opened properly!'

'Why doesn't he pull the cutaway?' yelled another.

'What the heck is *going on* over there?'

The crowd of paparazzi moved as one. Their giant lenses aimed at the sky like anti-aircraft weapons. Now the photographers saw it too – a second pilot zooming headfirst through the air, arms outstretched, straight as an arrow.

Sheer insanity.

The pilots collided. Together, they fell. The second pilot's canopy opened.

Shutters clicked. There were gasps of awe. But Ben only really noticed one thing: the hotel's lightning rod.

They're going to get caught.

When it happened there was a collective sigh. Now what?

Caroline's hand found Ben's. Without a word, she took his camcorder. She trained it on the hanging parachutists. He watched her zoom in as close as possible. The tiny screen suddenly encapsulated the struggle. Two people literally hanging by a thread.

He murmured, 'They're going to fall.'

Another voice in the crowd said, 'No. That parachute's caught up pretty good. They'll be OK. The firemen will get them.'

Jason Truby looked intently at Ben's mother. 'What does the boss say?'

That's right, Ben thought. *Mum's the boss of Carrington, now.* This would all land at her feet.

He lowered his gaze. Suddenly the act of looking up gave him vertigo. When he did, he wasn't sure if he saw the hotel of glass and concrete scraping the sky, or the jagged, snow-capped peaks from which his father had fallen a week earlier. He glanced at Caroline and felt sure he recognised the same painful memory in her expression.

The cry went round: 'Someone's called the fire services!'

Ben said, 'They're only fifteen metres off the edge of the summit pyramid. Any mountain-rescue crew could get them, no problem.'

Caroline studied the zoomed-in image. Her voice trembled a little. 'I don't think they have very long.'

'Why not?' Truby asked.

Caroline glanced at him but instead of replying she made an abrupt turn. One second later, she was running for the hotel's lobby.

Truby stared at Ben, puzzled. 'Where'd she go?'

Ben frowned in thought. Then his eyes widened as he realised. 'You are *not* serious. Mum!' He chased after Caroline, whose white-linen-clad figure had already disappeared into the cool marble lobby of the interior.

He finally caught up with his mother on the fifth floor. She was slamming the door of their suite as she left. In her right hand was the rucksack she'd used during their climbing week in the Himalayas.

Ben's heart pounded, hard.

She can't be serious.

When she saw him, Caroline didn't slow down. Rapidly, she strode to the lift and punched the 'UP' button.

'You are *not* . . .' Ben started.

But she looked at him, exasperated. 'Did you even hear the fire services? As if those poor people have the luxury of time.'

'Will you listen for a minute?'

'Ben – that second pilot risked her life. Did you see? There wasn't anything wrong with her plane. Now she's the only thing that's keeping the other one from falling. You must know I can't just stand by and watch.'

Ben paused, confused for a second. 'The girl pilot jumped? How d'you know it was her?'

'I recognised her plane. She risked her life for her partner. We can't let them die.'

The lift door opened. They stepped inside.

Caroline began to pull her flowing linen shirt over her head. Ben turned to face the wall, watching the floor numbers increase as the lift soared towards the summit.

Caroline dressed quickly in green soft-shell climbing shorts with a belt, rock shoes and the white vest she'd worn beneath her day clothes. She began fastening a metal ascender, Prusik cord and micropulley to her rope, and a shunt and a stop to her belt. She fixed a loose loop of climbing rope to her belt and attached tools to a carabiner near her right hip.

Ben watched in silence. Any second now the lift doors would open. Then it would begin. His mother would walk into a life-changing situation. Their entire future would be up for grabs.

He knew better than to plead with Caroline Brandis-Carrington. He knew why she was doing this. He doubted that anything he said would change her mind. It was what she'd done for five years in her twenties, before her marriage to Casper: mountain rescue.

Last week, Caroline might have saved his father.

If he'd held on for even three minutes longer...

Ben took a deep breath. Quietly he said, 'What can I do to help?'

Caroline glanced up in surprise. She smiled. 'OK. Good.'

The roof exit was guarded with dramatic signs that said, in Arabic and English, NO EXIT: EXTREME DANGER OF FALLING. Ignoring them, she climbed the flight of steps that led up to the sliding glass door.

Ben stood on the bottom step for a second. He watched his mother rope herself to the chunky, D-shaped metal door handle on the underside of the ceiling hatch. Then she moved out of sight. He followed, up the stairs.

Ben poked his head through the opening. The view was enough to still his breathing. The sky burned white in the dazzle of the sun. Beyond the concrete oasis of the city, a grey desert stretched across the horizon. To the south, over Hodariyat Island and towards the deep blue of the Persian Gulf, he saw a column of black smoke rising: the burning debris of the crashed display aircraft.

He could just see the two parachutists, dangling about twenty metres across and up from the door.

Caroline was standing less than two metres away. She handed Ben a spare loop of rope and a climbing belt. 'Fasten yourself to this door. Don't come out until you're fixed up.'

He nodded. So, there was going to be no argument about whether he participated, just action. *Good.*

Ben removed his jacket, folded it once and placed it on the carpeted floor. Then he knotted one end of the rope to the door handle, just as his mother had done. With practised fingers he fastened the climbing belt around his waist and threaded the narrow spool of rope through the stop that was attached to the belt. If the worst happened, the stop would hold him.

Warily, Ben stepped onto the ledge. His mother was already ten metres along. She'd flung her rope and its anchor at the base of the lightning rod and he could see the anchor gripped between two metal bars. Caroline was testing her weight on the rope. Ben swallowed. He forced himself to glance down. Softly, he swore and hurriedly looked back up.

The first pilot lay cradled in the arms of the second, the woman who'd jumped out of the display plane to catch him. Ben guessed he had to be unconscious. He didn't envy that guy the shock he'd get if he opened his eyes any time soon. But when he looked closely at the second pilot, his pulse began to race. His mother was right – they were almost out of time. The second pilot's expression was strained, eyes wide, and she altered her grip on her partner every few seconds, as though her arms were tiring.

Caroline leaned back on the rope, hard, opening up a V-shaped section of the city below between her body and the slope of the glass. Ben was transfixed. The reality was beginning to hit him: if this went badly, he'd end up an orphan, twice bereaved within a fortnight.

She was climbing the glassy slope now, using the ascender against a Prusik hitch and micropulley. Ben's eyes went to the two dangling pilots. He could just see the closed eyes of the first, unconscious one. Behind, the smaller second pilot's eyes were desperate and pleading.

'I'll get into position to catch her,' he called to Caroline, who simply nodded, focused on her own progress up the slope.

Ben edged further out onto the ledge, which was about a metre wide. There was no guard rail, nothing to stop him falling if he slipped. The drop was almost unfathomable. Yet he'd calmly faced similar heights in the Himalayas.

It's all in the prep. I know my belt and rope are good, he told himself.

Trapped climbers tended to be least vocal when they were closest to death. The female pilot had to be approaching the end of her energy reserves. The guy she was holding on to was at least thirty kilos heavier than her. Ben guessed that, by now, she was barely holding on to her team-mate.

Caroline was within two metres of the suspended pilots. He watched them exchange words. Over the next minute she fastened a harness and a second rope around the unconscious pilot. Now the man was tethered both to the metallic base of the lightning rod and to the handle of the roof exit.

At least if the unconscious pilot fell now, the worst thing that could happen to him – if his heart didn't give up the ghost – was that he'd dangle between two ropes until someone hauled him in. Nothing too catastrophic.

But, on the other hand, now a third person was roped to that door handle. Ben stole another look at it. It looked sturdy enough to hold a person. He wasn't sure about three. Better hope they wouldn't put it to the test.

His mother buckled slightly as the second pilot's weight was transferred to her. She leaned her weight against the unconscious pilot and the slope. Slowly, she began to descend, with the roped-up pilot slung partially over her left shoulder.

Ben tugged on his own rope. It felt well secured. He edged out until he was directly beneath his mother. He could hear her gasping with the effort of her descent.

'How are you doing?' she called down to him.

Ben turned his back on the gaping fall, braced his feet against the edges of the ledge and looked up. 'Go for it!'

Caroline lowered the unconscious pilot. Ben put his hands out to catch the man as he came within reach.

Then it happened. The pilot began to regain consciousness. He opened his eyes. What he saw must have sent a shockwave through his entire body because he snapped straight and instantly became a rigid, unwieldy rod.

The force of the jolt made a length of the rope slip through Caroline's fingers. The next thing Ben knew, the pilot was heading straight at him, fast.

Hands outstretched, Ben managed to block the man's fall, but the sudden weight was too much. Balanced on the edge of the skyscraper, Ben's feet slipped from under him and he went over, sliding down the side with a sickening squeal of rubber against glass.

Ben clutched the edge with his left hand, pressing

hard against the pilot's back with his right and forcing the man back onto the ledge.

But the fingers of his left hand began to falter.

He heard Caroline yell, 'Let go, Ben, I've got him!'

Gratefully, Ben removed his right hand and scrambled to get a solid grip on the edge of the building.

To his horror, he realised he couldn't.

The smooth surface of the building began to slide beneath his fingers. His right hand flapped uselessly in the wind. The only thing he could grab on to was the pilot. So he did – and immediately felt the man's body begin to slide off the edge. Heard his mother scream out, 'Ben!'

She couldn't take his weight as well as the pilot's. Ben knew if he didn't let go he'd pull them all over the edge.

I'm on a rope. It has to be me.

Ben unclenched his fingers.

Too distracted to yell, he fell in total silence.

⟵ VERTIGO ⟶

Dangling upside down on the end of a rope, Ben Carrington forgot how to breathe.

The air stilled in his throat. His eyes could take only a single second of what lay below: the plunging line of the Sky-High Hotel.

Three hundred metres straight down.

Smooth contours of silver and white swept into an almost graceful skirt at the base. To his right and left, competing structures rose out of the ground and rushed towards him, stopping tantalisingly short. At this height there was nothing but the whipping of the air at his face, shifting shadows on the ground below and grey roads crawling with tiny metal beetles.

Impossible distance.

The rope on which he dangled suddenly lurched – as though it were gradually tearing and he were being lowered slowly to the point of breakage.

He stared up at the rope in abject terror, utterly helpless as it lengthened. Then he stopped moving once more. Ben hung in an oasis of quiet, his neurons stalled by shock. Gradually they returned with a whoosh of sensation.

Ben shut his eyes, but the images were already etched

onto his retinas. Even behind his eyelids, he saw the void. In his right ankle he felt the unrelenting bite of the rope, mercilessly tight – the weight of his body focused on that one point. Despite the sensation of having his leg slowly dragged out of its hip socket, Ben allowed himself one thought, *Mountaineers face this every day. You're roped up. You're safe.*

His chest expanded rapidly as he drew a sudden deep breath. Then another.

The voice of his mother began to cut across the white noise of his thoughts. 'Don't swing.'

Ben tried to lift his head up enough so that he could see her face. The movement caused him to swing slightly. He heard his mother shout another warning. He relaxed. Upside down, suspended hundreds of metres above the skirt of glass, his hands felt tingly. If he fell he'd slice right through that glass. If the impact didn't kill him (surely it would?), he'd fly through whatever was in that room. He'd injure anyone inside. Maybe even kill them.

He drew another breath. The air on his cheek felt salty. Far above and to the east, the Airbus A380 roared as it approached for another pass. He opened his eyes to look. And shut them again.

The view was almost physically painful. The urge to shout for help almost irresistible. But he held on. Horrendous as it was to dangle headfirst over the lip of the Sky-High, Ben told himself that of the four people on the summit of the hotel, there were others in worse danger than he.

So long as he kept his eyes tightly shut, he could imagine it was nothing worse than a dodgy rock ledge and, any minute now, his mother would be sending a second rope down, or an ascender on his own rope.

You're roped up. You're safe. Don't swing.

Ben could feel his ribcage straining against his muscles. Upside down, the forces of gravity were exerting new and interesting sensations. He cracked open an eye, searching for his mother. She was still backing up along the ledge, dragging the prone body of the male pilot after her. Any minute now, she'd reach the door.

Then he realised the problem – and the reason why he'd felt that extra metre or so of give in his own rope. Ben's weight had pulled the roof exit shut.

He'd effectively trapped them all on top of the Sky-High.

'Don't swing! Relax!' his mother shouted down.

Ben nodded. A useless gesture, he realised, since Caroline probably couldn't spare him a glance.

'O … K.' It was all the sound he could force out.

There was something horribly fascinating about swinging headfirst, three hundred metres above Abu Dhabi. Once he'd managed to still the initial panic reflex; once he'd managed to believe that he wasn't going to simply plunge to his death, Ben realised that his mind wasn't able to take in the altitude.

It was just unreal, and bizarrely unlike what he'd experienced in the mountains. He gazed around and, this time, when the urge came to screw his eyes tightly closed, Ben managed to resist. He exhaled. He was alive. One day he might even get to where he knew his mother already was, when it came to heights: fearless.

Ben breathed in and out, circular breathing just the way he'd been taught: in through the nose and out, slowly, through pursed lips. The thudding noise of blood rushing in his eardrums began to subside. Far below him, Abu Dhabi was a toytown. A mirage.

The rope. The ledge. That's all there is.

The cord was biting into his ankle. He peered up along the rope, trying to work out what had happened up there, just before he'd slipped. It seemed that his foot had become caught in a loop. The length of rope between his belt and his foot was about two metres. He realised he could use it to pull himself upright. The extra force would hurt his ankle, no doubt about it, but at least he'd be doing something and not just hanging around like a dead weight.

Ben began to climb, hand over hand, up the rope between his belt and his trapped foot. With every movement the rope cut a little harder into his ankle. He could feel the tissue throbbing. He pushed the sensation out of his mind for a moment, concentrated instead on the air currents wafting him this way and that.

After a few minutes, he was almost perpendicular to the rope. He stretched, felt his fingers touch the tip of his Vans trainer. Amazingly, it was still in place.

As Ben reached forwards again, he felt himself begin to swing. Every movement was amplified by the wind as it gusted about him. His pulse rate soared once again. Fear gripped him hard in the chest and guts. He exhaled, trying to calm himself as before.

This had to work.

He tried to grab his foot and missed. He swung harder. He wriggled, trying to pull his foot free. The trainer was making the task more difficult. If he could lose the shoe, maybe he could twist free of the looped rope.

'You're swinging,' Caroline commented. He could tell she was trying to be helpful. Ben peered up. His mother was directly above him now. In a calm, encouraging voice she called, 'How's it going down there?'

The everyday tone of her voice was instantly soothing. He squinted in the sunlight. 'Your flyboy got a bit twitchy for a minute.'

'I'm sorry about that,' Caroline said, warmly. 'Need any help?'

'I'm good,' he grunted, pulling himself a little higher. 'Relax. Save the girl.'

Another voice said in an American accent, 'The "girl" is doing fine by herself, thanks.'

Ben saw his mother's head snap around. She was clearly astonished to find the female pilot approaching. The American had evidently cut herself free from the chute. He glanced along the glass pyramid – so blue from this angle that it almost merged with the sky – and saw that she must have lowered herself along the now-taut rope to which her colleague was attached.

Arms planted firmly on her hips, the pilot stared down at Ben. She was slender, fair-skinned with high cheekbones, almond-shaped eyes and a mop of bobbed, dark brown hair. But the most noticeable thing about her was a mischievous expression.

'That's a pretty crazy kid you got there,' she said to Caroline. 'Brave, sure, but kinda dumbass.'

Caroline's face flashed with annoyance. Ben felt his cheeks turning red with embarrassment. This was in danger of being humiliating. There was no way he was going to let this joker make fun of him when he'd practically got himself back to safety without help.

'Keep your hair on,' he said through gritted teeth. 'I'm fine.'

The female pilot merely chuckled.

Before she could do or say anything else, Ben lunged one last time. This time he was successful. He grabbed hold of his trainer. A few seconds later he'd worked the rope across the shoe. His foot was free. Now, with both feet braced against the vertical surface of the Sky-High Hotel, he began to climb.

The effort made sweat trickle down the back of his neck. He couldn't spare a single breath. A couple of wrenching minutes passed. His eyes were on the female pilot the whole time. When she threw down a hand to help him up the final bit, he didn't refuse.

She grinned at him. 'Kid, you're on a roll today.'

Breathing heavily, Ben nodded at the other pilot. 'Your mate isn't looking so good. Is he still alive?'

The young woman replied with another cheery grin. 'Shay? He fainted during the fall. Dude needs to see a doctor. My guess – it's his blood pressure. I told him to get checked out. Health checks aren't nearly regular enough – seems to me this display team is run like amateur hour. An accident was bound to happen.'

Caroline wiped a hand across her brow. In a weary, ragged voice she said, 'For heaven's sake, don't tell that to the insurers. Those lost planes are going to cost someone a fortune.'

⟵ TERRA FIRMA ⟶

The feel of solid matter beneath him was pure heaven.
The shrill sound of sirens could just be heard echoing
from the ground below. They felt very distant.

Caroline remarked, 'The cavalry's here.'

Ben sat up. For a few seconds, he just enjoyed the
sensation of being still, feeling the wind across his face
and in his hair, absorbing the moment. When he glanced
at her, the female pilot was gazing directly at him with
an expression of amused curiosity. Her face had an elfin
quality, almost boyish. He guessed that she was probably
older than she looked – maybe in her late twenties.

'So, you're Benedict?'

'Call me Ben.'

'I'm Addison Nicole Dyer. Friends call me Addi.'

'And blokes you make fun of for being on the end
of a rope – what do they call you?'

She smirked. 'Ha ha.'

Ben looked down. The vast distance to the city below
swam back into view. For a second he felt nauseous.

Addison Nicole said, 'You OK?'

He nodded. 'Yeah.' She was examining him with a
nonchalance that made him feel envious. It didn't seem
to bother her that they were perched on a ledge, three

hundred metres above the streets of Abu Dhabi. On an impulse, he blurted, 'Hey, lend me your phone. I left mine inside.'

Addison frowned slightly, but she reached into her jacket pocket and removed the phone. Ben took it from her fingers with a grin. 'Let's take a quick selfie. On top of the hotel – you, me and Mum.'

There was a reluctant smile in Addison's reply. 'Your friends will just love that, huh?'

'Too right.'

Ben put an arm around Addison's shoulders, held the phone in front of them and grinned widely into the lens. 'There. Just got you in that shot, Mum,' he said cheekily as he sent the image to his own mobile.

Caroline ignored the comment. 'Ben, Addison and I will pass Shay across to you, once you're standing on the stairs inside. Do you feel ready to support his weight? He's about eighty-five kilos.'

'No prob.'

Within a few minutes, Ben was inside and easing Shay to the floor. When Shay's head touched the carpet, his eyes opened. For a brief instant he stared at Ben, then closed his eyes again.

Addison was next through the hole in the ceiling. She squatted down beside his head. 'Hey, buddy. You almost checked out on me back there.'

Shay merely shook his head.

The lift door opened and three uniformed firemen burst through. When they saw Shay on the floor, one of them began to unfurl a rolled-up stretcher, while another sprang open a folded gurney. The lead fireman made straight for the stairs to the roof, but stopped when Caroline stepped through.

In excellent English, with a touch of a Middle Eastern accent, he said, 'Anyone else out there?'

'No, all present and accounted for,' Caroline replied.

The fireman nodded, clearly uncomfortable. 'Good job, ladies,' he said, a little gruffly, to Addison and Caroline. 'Excellent work. Your husbands will be most proud of you.'

'My husband fell off a mountain in the Himalayas a week ago,' Caroline said. There was frost in her tone. 'And I don't believe that Miss Dyer has a husband. Would that be right, Miss Dyer?' She turned to the female pilot, eyes wide.

The pilot followed her lead. 'That's correct, ma'am. It's just little ol' me.'

Their pointed tone made no impression whatsoever on the fireman. He merely gazed in fresh awe at Caroline. 'Your husband is ... Casper Carrington?'

Ben watched Addison pick up on this information.

She looked from Ben to Caroline. 'You're Benedict ... and Caroline Carrington?'

Caroline removed a climbing glove and offered her hand. 'It's Brandis-Carrington,' she said. 'Pleased to properly meet you, Miss Dyer.'

The pilot replied, 'Just Addison, ma'am. Or Addi. And I owe you one for getting my ass off that pyramid. I can't say as I'd have lasted long enough for you fine gentlemen to get to Shay in time.' This last line was delivered with a sly glance at the lead fireman.

'I was just fortunate enough to be on-site,' Caroline replied with a smile.

Addison continued, 'So is this your deal, then – mountain rescue?' She gestured to Ben and then Caroline.

Ben chuckled. 'Us? Ha, not exactly. We were winging it.'

'Really? Your mom seemed like a pro.'

'I was, once,' Caroline said.

'I guess you don't exactly need to work. But if you ever did, you'd make an awesome rescuer.'

'Maybe we should start our own agency,' Ben said with a grin.

'Hmm,' Caroline mused, looking thoughtful. Then to the fireman she said, 'Now, how is Mr Shay? Will he be all right, do you think?'

One of the firemen who'd just finished lifting Shay onto the gurney glanced up. 'His blood pressure is low, but that's normal after a thing like this. The paramedics are in the next lift.'

Caroline put a hand on Addison's shoulder and drew her to one side with Ben. 'That was quite an impressive stunt, Addison.'

'Oh, it's not that much. I used to do a lot of skydiving, when I was training for the Air Force. It can get kind of addictive.'

Ben said simply, 'It was *immense*.'

'But, Ben, I can admit this now. You almost gave me a heart attack,' said Caroline.

He didn't know what to say.

'Kid, you ever stand on a three-hundred-metre ledge before?' Addison asked.

'Plenty of times.'

Addison turned to Caroline. 'Sheer drop, smooth building, urban setting – unless you're seriously cool with altitudes, that stuff will knock the brave outta most anybody. Your boy did OK.'

Caroline nodded once, her expression serious as she absorbed the judgement. 'You're right. But still, Ben, I shouldn't have let you go out there.'

'You needed me.'

'No. It was wrong to involve you.'

'You showed a lot of guts out there, Benedict Carrington,' said Addison.

The blush that crept over Ben then had nothing to do with shame.

The lift doors opened again. Three paramedics crowded round Shay. A fourth came over to where Ben was standing. He cast a glance over Addison, then Caroline and, finally, Ben.

'No injuries?'

'A bit of rope burn, that's all,' Ben told him.

The hotel security had prevented anyone else from taking the lifts up. For a few precious moments, Ben, Caroline and Addison were able to enjoy the quiet rush of relief as one of the paramedics handed out bars of Lindt milk chocolate 'for the shock'.

As he bit into the chocolate, Ben realised with a jolt that since he'd stepped into the lift with his mum he hadn't thought about his father. He hesitated to mention this to his mother, but decided to risk it. They'd shared so much of their grief thus far. It seemed wrong to keep this to himself.

Yet when he told her, a curious shadow seemed to cross her face. 'You stopped thinking about him? Good. I'm glad you managed to find some distraction.'

The bitterness in her voice took him by surprise. He wished he hadn't raised the subject.

'You ... you didn't ... get distracted?'

Caroline fixed him with cool, blue-grey eyes. 'How could I? For a few moments there, I thought I was going to lose my son in just the same way.'

Ben felt the milk chocolate clogging up his throat. 'I'm sorry.'

'You misunderstand. I'm not blaming *you*, Ben.'

Instantly, he understood. She was blaming herself. 'No. Mum, I'm not having that.'

'I didn't train you enough.'

'But we weren't expecting to do this.'

She nodded. Her mind seemed to drift elsewhere for a moment. 'That's true. That was the mistake.' Then her gaze snapped back to his. 'We'd really have to do something about that.'

'We'd have to do something about that … if *what*?' Ben demanded.

'If we had our own rescue agency,' she said, simply.

At the time, her statement didn't properly register with Ben. All he saw was that colour had begun to return to his mother's cheeks and she seemed filled with a new confidence. It was noticeable from the moment that she stepped out of the lift and back into the lobby of the Carrington Sky-High, which had been hastily prepared for the press to greet her. It was in the way she moved.

As they strolled across the floor, which was tiled with huge squares of two subtly distinct types of Italian marble, the lobby flared with the light of dozens of cameras flashing. Ben slowed his walk, smiled awkwardly as voices urged, 'Ben! Ben! Over here! Smile, Benedict! How'd it feel when you were hanging over the edge?'

The sheer weight of their collective gaze knocked all confidence from him – but not from his mother. Ben watched, slightly dazed, as she strolled casually to a podium that had been erected next to the white grand piano.

Speaking into the microphone she began, 'Thank you.'

Caroline's next words were lost in heartfelt cheers and the roar of applause.

The computerised voice was just a little too cheerful for the words it spoke. '*The human is not breathing.*'

Rigel, a flat-coated retriever dog, gazed up at Ben from the untidy front lawn of the boy's grandfather's Austrian manor house. Around his neck was a metallic PVC collar with flaps that dropped down on both sides of his head. Ben held one part of the collar firmly between the fingers and thumb of his right hand.

'That's what happens if Rigel bites this sensor on the high-tech collar. We train him which sensor to bite down on. There are different ones. Each one gives a different response. It's kind of like teaching him to talk. The voice is a bit perky, though.'

Ben released the sensor. Rigel's tongue dangled from his mouth. His tail wagged. Ben glanced at the dog harness in his hands. It was probably similar enough to Rigel's old blind-guide harness to make the dog think he was being called back into action.

Caroline put her head on one side. 'Impressive. I think I'd prefer a voice with a different accent too, not so American.'

Ben put the modified harness back into its box. Earlier that morning, while his mother had been walking in the nearby alpine meadows, he'd fielded three successive calls from the Chief Finance Officer at Carrington International. He was supposed to pass on a message. He'd even written it down.

Then the parcel with Rigel's collar embedded with wearable computer technology had arrived. It had demanded Ben's immediate attention. The CFO from Carrington International was already fading into irrelevance. Ben made a mental note to tell Caroline about the call, when they'd finished talking about Rigel.

'You don't like Rigel as an American?'

'Papa wouldn't have approved,' she said, wryly. 'Ever the Anglophile. He'd prefer the voice of an Old Kentonite, like your father. Or you, but that would probably be somewhat confusing. Ben, it's a nice toy but what's the purpose here?'

Ben frowned. 'I thought you'd be more enthusiastic. We were lucky to get one of these high-tech collars — the orders are backed up for a year.'

'Perhaps if I understood what point you're trying to make?'

Firmly he told her, 'I think Rigel can be useful to our rescue outfit.'

'*My* mountain-rescue outfit, don't you mean?' she said, with a smile and gently teasing tone. 'Hey, we're called the Caroliners, by the way.'

She pronounced it German-style, *Caroleeners*, like her own name.

'The *Caroliners*?'

'To rhyme with *carabiners*.'

'Seriously?' he said in a level voice. 'Hilarious.'

She smiled. 'I thought you'd appreciate it.'

'What's with "*my* rescue outfit", anyhow?'

'Ah, well,' Caroline gave an elegant shrug, 'I'm going to have to forge ahead on my own for a while, I think.'

Ben paused. This didn't sound like a joke.

'Because of what happened at the Sky-High?' Ben asked, incredulous. 'But I was all right! I self-rescued.'

She nodded, totally serious. 'Yes, you did. And I felt sick, watching you. Physically ill. Your father's accident has turned me into an anxious parent.'

Ben was quiet for a few moments, trying to absorb what she was telling him.

Meanwhile, Caroline continued, 'I think we need someone bigger. Stronger. More experienced. A mountain man. Dieter from the village. Or that man everyone uses for going up the Holzgauer ... Jurgen.'

Ben stroked Rigel's head, thinking. Her logic was sound, but he didn't like being excluded from something so exciting. The dog lay between Ben's knees, licking his hand every now and again and gazing hopefully into his eyes. 'What about the dog? You need Rigel. And Rigel needs me.'

'Why do I need Rigel?'

'I can re-train him,' Ben said. 'He was a pretty good guide dog for your dad but, at heart, he's a gun dog, a retriever.'

Caroline looked amused. 'Is this some roundabout way of asking me to let you take up shooting?'

'Blatantly not! But if Rigel has the instinct to fetch shot game, we can use that to have him find people who are lost on the slopes. He's strong, he's light, he's fast. And with this wearable tech, I can train him to tell you things about the condition of the person in trouble.'

' "The human is not breathing". Is that what you mean?'

'It's useful, right? Rigel could get to someone ahead of the rescuers. He could let you know stuff in advance.'

Despite herself, Caroline seemed to hesitate. She crouched down on the grass, ran a hand over Rigel's head and throat. The dog was clearly delighted at the attention and began to wag his tail, making tiny high noises in his throat as he leaned into Caroline's affectionate rubbing.

'Is that something you'd like to do, boy? Be Ben's rescue buddy? Wear a science-fiction collar and talk American?'

'He'd love to,' Ben said. 'It wouldn't have to be risky, Mum. I don't have to do rope work right away, but I want to help.'

She stood up. 'Well ...'

'Yeah ...?'

'I'm going to need a demonstration.'

He nodded, fervently. 'Totally.'

'I left a sweater in the meadow on my walk this morning. It's quite high up; I took the ski-lift. Rigel should be able to pick up the scent at the water trough near the village shop – I stopped there and leaned over to get a drink.'

'You want me to fetch the sweater?'

She gave an enigmatic smile. 'I'd like Rigel to find it.'

Eagerly, Ben rose to his feet, the calls from Carrington International entirely forgotten, along with the urgent message he was supposed to pass on – that they needed to know when Mrs Carrington could attend a board meeting.

Ben went to the boot room and located Rigel's lead as well as his own hiking rucksack. He rinsed out the water bottle and refilled it, checked that the emergency rope and climbing belt were there. He went to the kitchen, made peanut-butter sandwiches and took a bar of milk chocolate from the box where his mother kept the biscuits. He added a handful of dog treats to a sandwich bag and stuffed it into the pocket of his North Face jacket. Then he changed into his Hi-Tec hiking boots, whistled for Rigel and set off.

The village was a fifteen-minute walk from his late grandfather's partially restored 'schloss'. The word meant 'castle' in German, but really the house was not much more than a good-sized, stone-built manor house surrounded by some once-beautiful gardens. Prior to the Nazi occupation of Austria that had begun before the Second World War, the grounds would have been crawling with gardeners and groundskeepers. Inside, domestic staff would have cooked and cleaned and waited upon his grandfather, the count.

There were photos of Ben's grandfather as a boy, looking like a little prince in his realm. But the moment the 'Bavarian thugs' of the German National Socialist Party had marched into Austria, the family's fortunes had changed. By the time the Nazis had arrived to commandeer Schloss Bach for their own officers, the Brandis family had gone – joining the many who'd taken trains to Switzerland and then to England. By the time Ben's grandfather had returned in the 1970s, the family fortune was gone – the house ransacked and burned in the final weeks of the war. The villagers still spoke darkly of those times. Most referred to the family's 'honourable exile', but a few – those who'd shared the Nazis' murderous prejudices – muttered about 'treachery'.

Maybe those hateful people had set fire to Schloss Bach. To this day, no one knew who'd done it.

Ben's grandfather had returned alone, the sole survivor of his family. He'd set about the business of marrying and raising a young family, and put his own sweat into the restoration of the estate. The villagers had watched in growing admiration as the young Count Brandis became the first labourer on his own land.

Ben wasn't sure what he'd do, in the same situation. Family traditions were important, but a house like Schloss Bach could be a millstone. It had certainly been that for most of his grandfather's life. Now that the house was hers, his mother seemed determined to follow her father's instinct to preserve. With Carrington cash, the place would finally be restored to magnificence – a suitable base for the country's newest alpine-rescue service.

It would be a whole new lease of life for his mother. Yet, despite this exciting new venture, it seemed pretty clear that Ben's life wouldn't change. Within ten days he'd be back at school, in Oxfordshire, England. Back to hitting the books. To prep, curfew and no girls.

He found the cattle water trough just outside the village. He gave the dog a woollen mitten that Caroline had first wiped across her own face. Rigel sniffed the mitten hard, tail wagging as he recognised the scent. Ben steered Rigel towards the base of the trough.

'Ceecee, Rigel. She's in trouble. Find Ceecee.'

Rigel pulled at the lead, energetically urging Ben into the field. Ben kept directing him back to the trough. It was no good – Rigel just became more and more adamant. At full tension, the dog was almost stronger than Ben.

Curious to see what Rigel would do, Ben let him off his lead. Rigel immediately scampered around in delight, sniffing the meadow at the edges of the road. He spent at least five minutes building a total scent-map of the region.

Ben leaned against the trough, bored. He took out his mobile phone. There were a couple of messages from school-friends. They lived in London and were having a brilliant final week of the summer holiday. If his father hadn't died, Ben would now be partying with those boys and their network of London-based teenage girls from similar public schools. He'd have been almost totally at liberty.

He felt a creeping guilt. So much of what he missed about his father was wrapped up in the life Casper Carrington had made possible for Ben. Did that make Ben a bad person?

The truth was that he'd barely known his father. Living mainly in Austria with his mother during the holidays and at school during terms, there just hadn't been an opportunity for Ben to get to know his father well. Running Carrington International had taken up all of Casper's time. At least, it had felt that way to Ben.

When Rigel began to bark, Ben looked up. The dog had wandered into the meadow and was urging Ben to follow. He could see a faint path in the long, wildflower-dappled grass. It led beyond the village and to the mountain path above. Ben gazed at the pinkish-grey granite of the mountain beyond the treeline. There was grass almost all the way up to the summit.

His mother had said she'd taken the gondola, but that didn't make sense – Rigel was leading Ben into the meadow, to the walking path. The cable cars all left from a chalet-style building at the other end of the village.

Ben brought up his mother's contact details on his mobile phone and called.

'Are you sure you took the gondola?' he asked.

'Yes.'

'Then I don't get it. Rigel's gone into the meadow.'

'And?'

'Well – it's like you didn't take the lift.'

Caroline sounded amused. 'Who are you going to believe? Your mother or a dog?'

'But … Rigel *can't lie*, Mum. That's the point. That's why he's useful. People can be mistaken. Dogs don't lie.'

'Ah. You have a point.'

Ben punched the air, flushed with success. Clearly Rigel had just passed Caroline's test with flying colours. Ben sensed his mother's objections to him and Rigel joining the team breaking down.

Caroline stood at the edge of the water, one hand warding off the low glare of the sun. From the middle of the lake, Ben waved.

Within the deep, forest-green water of the glacier lake, he shivered. It had taken him days of intense effort to persuade Rigel to immerse himself in the chilly waters. Today, for the first time, when Ben had begun his swim across the widest part of the lake, Rigel had clung to his side.

The water was still and crystal-clear for the first two metres. It reflected, with the clarity of a mirror, the pine forest that rose around its perimeter. In the centre, the depths turned into impenetrable green. Ben could feel the heat being sucked out of his body by the coolness around him. He moved steadily, his left wrist trailing the nylon tether that connected him to the light waterproof barrel that held his clothes. Sweeping the water from before him, he kept a vigilant eye on Rigel. They were about halfway across, a hundred metres still to go.

'All right, boy,' Ben said, soothingly. 'Ceecee's there. Can you hear? Ceecee.'

Rigel tasted the air, hopefully. He didn't take his gaze from Ben.

'Ceecee,' Ben repeated. 'Over there. Come on, Rigel. You can swim faster than this.'

Ben dipped his head in the water. He pulled away with a couple of strokes of crawl, then stopped and turned to watch Rigel. The dog had stopped. He was treading water. For a moment, Ben's stomach lurched. It was still quite a long way to shore. Until today, Rigel hadn't ventured more than ten metres from the edge. What if he froze with fear, fought Ben off from trying to drag him to safety? Rigel would drown for sure.

Ben swam slowly back to Rigel. The plastic barrel bobbed in the water, trailing him. He could hear his own heart thumping now. In the outdoors, a situation could suddenly turn dangerous. They were in the middle of the lake, but Rigel still wanted to return the way they'd come.

Ben held onto one of Rigel's front paws. 'Ceecee,' he said, in a voice of practised authority. 'Go to Ceecee.'

Rigel threw one final glance over his shoulder at the shore from which they'd started. He didn't look at the shore in front of them, only at Ben.

Ben released Rigel's paw. Shivering, he put his face close so that the dog could lick and smell him. He rubbed the side of his head against Rigel's ear. 'Come on, pooch,' he murmured. 'You can do this. I remember my first time. It's hard, but it's just swimming. Swimming and more swimming. And then you're there.'

He began to move forwards again, slowly. This time, Rigel followed.

They reached the shore several minutes later. Ben wanted to throw his arms around Rigel and hug him, but the dog was too excited to be back on solid land, and to see Caroline. She had armed herself with a black bath sheet and was rubbing him dry.

'He did it,' Ben breathed. He unscrewed the lid from the watertight barrel he'd been dragging, removed Rigel's lead and handed it to Caroline. Then he pulled out a small hiking towel, his jeans, T-shirt and sandals. A few minutes later, Ben was more or less dry and dressed.

Caroline attached the lead to Rigel's collar, encouraging the dog's calm stance by offering him tiny pieces of cheese rind, which he chewed with obvious relish.

'So he's a water dog now,' she said with approval.

'Rigel is a water *boss*. Next time you leave him a sweater to track, you can leave it in water. He'll find it just fine.'

'He's found every trail I've left so far, so he might, at that.'

Ben took Rigel's lead from his mother's hand, bowing his head so that she wouldn't see the proud grin he just couldn't suppress.

They returned to Schloss Bach by car. On the way to his bedroom to change, Ben passed Addison in the hall, with the two local mountain men Jurgen and Dieter. They were sipping from glasses filled with Grüner Veltliner, a sweet Austrian wine. Addison looked slim and pretty in her neat, navy-blue shirt-dress. Both men were tall and fair-haired with lean, muscular builds. In their dinner jackets they looked fantastic next to Addison.

Caroline had bought a Robinson R66 helicopter and ordered a repaint job – bright orange. That was about it so far. The Caroliners weren't ready, but Ben guessed that this wasn't about to stop his mother from keeping the launch-party booking at the Krazy Korner nightclub.

After he'd showered, dressed in his own dinner jacket and moussed his light brown hair, everyone was ready. Caroline held an arm out to welcome Ben as he came down the main staircase into the hall.

She put her mouth close to his ear and said quietly, 'I'm so glad you're here to escort me.'

Ben stood a little taller, then.

The terrace of the Krazy Korner overlooked the ski slopes of St Anton am Arlberg, dominated by the massive peaks of the Kapall and Schindler mountains. When they arrived, the light of the setting sun was turning the snow-capped Tyrolean Alps a salmon shade of pink. The lights and tables of the bar were decorated in orange and black bunting. Caroline had arranged for orange disco lights to swirl as soon as the daylight faded.

Jurgen, Dieter and Addison disappeared into the bathrooms. Minutes later they emerged with orange-and-black jumpsuits covering their evening outfits. Even with the extra bulk of their dinner suits, the crew looked fit and ready for anything.

Caroline beamed when she saw them. 'All set for the stunt?'

It wouldn't be as cool as the one Addison had managed to pull off at the Sky-High, Ben thought. But then what could possibly top that? Tonight, Addison was going to be flying the R66 helicopter; Jurgen and Dieter were going to do some rappelling. Ben was only there to escort Caroline and Rigel. He'd resigned himself to what was basically an onlooker role.

He checked his watch. A stickler for punctuality, Caroline had insisted that they arrive thirty minutes early. As ever, Ben had to watch Caroline being dragged into urgent discussions with the bar manager, then Jurgen, then Addison. After a few minutes, Ben turned back to his phone.

'I really must insist,' said an impatient voice.

Ben looked up. A woman with impeccably styled chestnut hair, wearing a tight-fitting, dark grey two-piece suit, had barged past the bar's security staff. She was standing over Caroline, who merely glanced at her, bewildered.

'I'll be with you in about five minutes, my dear,' the countess told the newcomer.

Clearly exasperated, the woman said, 'With respect, Mrs Carrington, it really has to be now!'

Caroline didn't even put down the A3-sized seating plan she was studying. She merely peered at the bar manager beside her. 'Can you see it?'

The bar manager took the paper from Caroline. 'I could put them both here,' he said, pointing.

The woman's jacket must have been really uncomfortable because she was shifting inside the garment as though it were filled with ants. She raised her voice, saying, 'Mrs Carrington, I appreciate that you're trying to give three people your attention. It is wasted effort, I can assure you. Right now, I'm the only one that counts.'

The bar manager as well as every member of his staff within earshot stared in amazement at the suited woman. Caroline herself did nothing except to lay the plan of the bar onto the table before her. With great deliberation, she turned her attention to the visitor.

'Please, can I help you?'

'I'm Marion Goring. I'm the chief financial officer of Carrington International.'

Caroline extended a wary hand. 'I'm terribly sorry, Ms Goring; I don't believe we've met.'

'Just once, Mrs Carrington. It was at the annual garden party in Bayswater, last year. I was head of accounts back then.'

'Really? What happened to Bradley Carlisle? Wasn't he CFO?'

'Mr Carlisle is gone,' Marion Goring snapped. 'I became CFO last month.'

Ben glanced at his mother. A new CFO within weeks of the chief executive's death? It didn't sound ideal. Much worse, though, was the fact that the news clearly came as a surprise to Caroline. What was going on?

Caroline rose slowly to her feet. If she was angry, she was managing to keep it completely under control. 'I don't believe I was informed of any of this.'

'That's correct. We wanted to clean house a little before we brought you in on the, ah, *details* of the changeover.'

'"Clean house"?' Caroline frowned.

Ben didn't know a huge amount about business, but this didn't sound good. 'Is this really the time and place?' he said to Goring. 'Can't you see my mum is busy? Why don't you make an appointment?'

'I've tried,' came the curt reply. 'On several occasions. Mrs Carrington, it seems, is rather preoccupied.'

'Her husband just died,' Ben said, coldly. 'What do you expect?'

Marion Goring continued. 'Indeed. I was at the funeral, although it seems you don't remember me.'

Ben felt himself grow tense. 'There were a lot of people at the funeral. Is this why you're being so weird?'

Caroline put a hand on his arm. 'It's all right, Ben. Ms Goring's obviously been through a bad time with the company. It's not surprising she's perturbed.' She turned to Goring. 'Are you part of Casper's succession plan? I'm very sorry, you're right, I haven't been keeping up enough. There's just been so much to do.'

'Regrettably, Mr Carrington didn't leave anything resembling a succession plan. The board should have obliged him to do so, in my opinion, but ...' Goring gave a dismissive shrug, '... they weren't keen on actions that were likely to irritate your husband.'

Now she stared Caroline directly in the eye in a way that Ben found suddenly unnerving.

Caroline took a half-step back, though she returned Marion's gaze with intense focus. 'Ms Goring, would you please come to the point?'

The woman placed a blue box file on the table in front of Caroline.

'Everything you need to know is in here.'

The air between the two women crackled with latent catastrophe. Caroline's feelings were absolutely reined in as she asked, very quietly, 'And *what* is in here?'

'Everything you need in order to understand. The money – it's gone. There's nothing left. Casper was an incompetent surrounded by fools and – I'm sorry to say this – by crooks. Bradley Carlisle was embezzling from the company. It's complicated. We're going to need a few hours to go through it. Then I need you to come with me to meet the FCA.'

Ben said, 'What's the FCA?'

'The Financial Conduct Authority,' Goring replied. 'The people who police the banking system.'

An expression of dawning revelation, of illusions being cast away by a crushing truth, now overtook Caroline's face. Bitterly, she said, 'The Sky-High.'

Ben realised it the moment she spoke – his mother had known there was something wrong.

Goring nodded. 'Paying for the Sky-High has broken

Carrington International. The previous CFO, Bradley Carlisle, bribed every official in the chain – a chain that reaches from the United Arab Emirates, across Europe and all the way to St Petersburg. He borrowed and mortgaged everything. Concealed losses with creative accounting. Set up a whole separate system of finances that was hidden from everyone except Mr Carrington, from what I can tell.'

Ben felt as though all the blood had rushed out of his head. 'You're saying that my dad knew?'

'Mr Carrington had a plan and his backers had faith in him. Unfortunately, without him, that is gone.'

Bewildered, Caroline said, 'And what about Mr Carlisle?'

Marion Goring shrugged. 'Vanished. Halfway to stay with one of his benefactors in the Georgian Republic, I shouldn't wonder. Most likely travelling under a false identity.'

His mother held and then released a ragged breath. She seemed unsteady. Ben couldn't stay silent any longer. 'Mum. What does this mean?'

But Goring answered his question, not Caroline. 'It means Carrington International is over,' she said with precision. 'I hope any assets you have are in your own name, Mrs Carrington, because the authorities are going to take *every penny*.'

━ SCHADENFREUDE ━

Kenton College was probably out of the question, now. Ben couldn't see his mother coughing up the thirty-odd-thousand pounds per year it would cost to send him back for sixth form.

His thoughts turned towards the army officer fitness test. Forty-four press-ups in two minutes. He could easily do thirty-five, right now. Just give it a couple of weeks and he'd ace it. Maybe it wasn't too late to apply for a scholarship at Welbeck Defence Sixth Form College.

Death *and* bankruptcy was a heavy load to absorb. But Ben was determined that it wouldn't be the end of his hopes and dreams. Plenty of people were broke. He heard it all the time – boys whose fathers had lost their jobs being taken out of school. Somehow, they survived.

Yet, from looking at his mother's collapsed shoulders, Ben guessed that bankruptcy might be more difficult for her to handle. *His* hopes were wrapped up with the British army. The UK government wasn't likely to close down the armed services anytime soon. New recruits were always needed. Caroline Brandis-Carrington, on the other hand, had invested all her energy – and all her future, Casper-less dreams – into the Caroliners.

Ben didn't want to ask the question but, without cash, how would the Caroliners ever get off the ground?

'Would you like us to take off the uniforms?' Jurgen asked. He touched Caroline's arm as he spoke, his voice full of concern.

Caroline shook her head. 'Out of the question. The party goes ahead as planned.'

Addison broke into a hopeful smile. 'Yay, Countess! Go, Caroliners!'

The bar manager gave a single nod, tapped a finger to his forehead in salute to Caroline. '*Ausgezeichnet, Frau Gräfin.*' He wandered into the interior, calling his staff around him.

'You let me worry about funding the Caroliners,' Caroline told Jurgen with a bright smile.

The mountain man grinned. Vigorously, he shook her hand. 'All right!' With Dieter, he returned to preparing for their rappelling stunt while Addison accepted the keys to the R66 that Caroline offered.

A moment later, Ben was alone with his mother. He couldn't quite understand her sudden burst of optimism. 'You've got some money stashed away?' he asked hopefully.

'Papa's house, that's mine. And the Caroliners are in my name. But that's all.'

'What about paying for school?'

She turned to him with a rueful grin. 'You don't get out of it that easily, I'm afraid. Your school fees come from a trust fund.'

'Oh,' he said. He wasn't sure if he was disappointed. At least that was some money that wouldn't be taken away. On the other hand, it meant his mother was right – getting out of school wouldn't be easy. 'But could you lose the house?'

Caroline heaved a lengthy sigh. 'It might come down to the house or the Caroliners. I already owe the builders so much.'

'Why the party, then?'

'Because, my dear, we have expectations to fulfil and people depending on us for a living. So we hold our heads up and get on with it. OK?'

'This is a nightmare. I'm sorry, Mum. We can't seem to catch a break.'

'Hey.' She pinched his cheek. 'You got knocked off that ridiculous hotel, but you climbed right back up. "Catch a break"? It seems to me that we already did.'

Her words were positive, yet Ben didn't miss the slump in her stance. Her aura of confidence, so radiant since that day on the Sky-High, seemed to have disappeared along with the Carrington fortune.

It was scary how much power was vested in such an abstract concept as money.

But the party preparations continued. As the sky began to darken, the air temperature plummeted and the bar staff switched on the gas-powered patio heaters and lit the candles in the cobalt-blue glass holders on each table.

Guests began to arrive. His mother had invited most

of their neighbours from the village, about a thirty-minute drive from St Anton. Then there was the press – a few key media contacts from Vienna.

Ben recognised a few other teenagers, kids he remembered from kindergarten before he'd been sent to prep school in London. They were friendly to him but vaguely cool and distant, as they had been for as long as he could remember. It was a fairly Austrian scene, all in all – apart from a couple of international visitors in the shape of Addison and her father, stepmother and younger sister.

Hours earlier, Ben had felt let down by the fact that not a single one of his school-friends had accepted their party invitations. They'd all been too busy with 'unmissable' social events in London. Now, however, he was relieved. He couldn't imagine how the Caroliners would survive, whatever his mother was saying. Ben could tell she was putting on an act. He'd come to know her stoic face rather well over the past few weeks.

This party was the last hurrah and Ben knew it.

He pulled away from the gathering crowd. He found an almost full bottle of Stiegl lager on a table, carefully wiped the open neck with his sleeve and took a sip. The bar staff had been instructed not to serve Ben alcohol, but he wasn't going to let that stop him. Not tonight. He went right to the edge of the balcony, gulping down more beer.

Life *sucked*. As he drank, he began to see things even more clearly. Why did his father have to die?

Ben had hoped that his dad's death would become easier to accept as time went by, yet it was only getting worse. Carrington's company had crumbled in less than two months. His mother had coped only by channelling her energy into the Caroliners. Now it looked as though she was going to lose even that.

It wasn't fair.

Caroline had taught Ben from very young not to say those words, not to even *think* them. 'If things were fair,' she would remind him, 'we'd be poor.'

Right now, however, he was finding them incredibly difficult to avoid.

'Where I come from, son, you have to be twenty-one to drink that.'

Ben swung round. He almost dropped the bottle over the edge of the balcony. Standing beside him was Jason Truby. Ben raised the bottle of lager in an ironic toast.

'I'm drinking to Fate. Everything is screwed,' he said, simply. There was no point lying.

Caroline hadn't mentioned that Truby might be coming. Ben, however, wasn't surprised. He'd been reading about the CEO of Trubycom. Turned out there was quite a lot to Truby's business life that Ben hadn't known.

The Fireflash XL5 chip, sure. Everyone knew about that. Almost every major mobile phone used the Fireflash. But Ben hadn't realised that Trubycom also had divisions involved in aviation, semi-conductors and, most bizarrely of all, drilling equipment. The company had offices all over the world, from what Ben could tell. Jason Truby, like Ben's father, was the kind of man who might show up anywhere on the planet.

Truby watched him for a moment. Gradually, he dropped the smile. 'The word is out about Carrington International.'

'What's going on? Tell me the truth,' Ben added, quickly. 'You might be the only person who will.'

'Ben, I only know what I'm hearing on the grapevine.'

'Did my dad break the law?'

Truby gave a terse nod. 'Maybe.'

'What happens next?'

'They'll investigate the whole board. Your mom seems likely to be in the clear, as far as the law goes, but if they find wrong-doing ... they could take it all.'

Ben said, 'So it's true.'

Truby didn't answer. He looked across to Caroline. Ben thought he could detect a certain longing in his gaze. Caroline seemed not to have noticed Truby's arrival. She was busy making pleasant chit-chat with Addison's family.

'A whole heap of trouble is about to fall all around your mom,' Truby reflected. 'And I'm telling you this, Ben, she's too good for that. Addison, too. Not one person in a billion would have done what they did at the Sky-High.'

'Yeah. So? That's life, isn't it? One day you're up and trying to help people. Next, it's all turned to ... well, you know, and people laugh at you. Like it's a joke.'

'Who's laughing? All I see is a bunch of people supporting your mother.'

'That Goring woman from the company. It was like
she enjoyed giving us the bad news. *Schadenfreude*, we
call it.'

'There can be a lot of untold rivalries in business. You
don't really know what's been going on at Carrington
International. Looks like no one does. Don't be bitter,'
Truby advised, 'it's not helpful. Or becoming.'

Ben ignored him. His eyes were hot with resentment.
'There are people here from the newspapers. Tomorrow
they'll print the photos, but they'll be sure to get a dig
in at my dad.'

'So what? You think your mom did what she did
for the audience? You think the Caroliners was about
getting her name into the papers?'

'Mum doesn't give a toss about any of that. She's
found something she's good at and she just wants to
help people. Not everyone can say that. Like Bill Gates,
what does he do ...?'

'He cures malaria,' Truby said, a little archly. 'No
biggie.'

'OK, so Gates does malaria. Mum, she wants to rescue
climbers. And skiers.'

'An inspirational project, in my opinion. Look around
you – most people here think so, too.'

Ben shrugged. 'Well, it's a party.'

Truby stared him evenly in the eye. 'You're being

maudlin. This doesn't seem like you, Ben. I'd say that beer doesn't agree with you.'

Ben felt distinctly uncomfortable. It was true – he was feeling angrier with every swallow. 'Why are you here, anyway?'

'Caroline asked me.'

'It's a long way to come,' Ben said, bluntly. 'Are you after her?'

Truby laughed. He seemed genuinely taken aback. 'That's quite a man-to-man question! Good, Ben. I like it. To tell the truth, I have a business proposition for the Caroliners. Seems to me, they'd make a great fit with something I've got going on of my own.'

Ben put down his bottle of lager. '*You've* got a rescue agency?'

'Don't sound so surprised. I was hoping you'd help me out.'

'Me, help you?'

'Yes, Ben. Maybe you can persuade your mom to take a little trip with me?' Truby looked at him, hard. 'I can't think of anyone whose opinion your mom would value more.'

'A trip where?'

'Near Cozumel, in the Mexican Caribbean. I've got a place there.'

'The Caribbean?' Ben's mood felt suddenly lighter. Eventually, he couldn't suppress a grin. 'You drive a hard bargain, Jason Truby. But if you insist.'

NEAR COZUMEL

They flew into a midnight-blue sky. The last rays of the golden-circle sun were behind them as the sun sank beyond the Mexican Caribbean's premier tourist island, Cozumel.

Ben shot a quick look at Truby, who was inscrutable behind dark Oakley sunglasses.

'Hey, I thought you said ...?'

'My place *near* Cozumel.' Truby pointed out to sea. 'Thataway.'

Sitting in the co-pilot seat, Ben watched as Truby's hands moved with smooth efficiency around the controls of the Sikorsky S-76 helicopter. He had to remind himself that the man next to him had been the planet's first civilian to step onto another world – the asteroid *1036 Ganymed* – even if that 'world' was merely a hunk of rock whose diameter was just shy of thirty-five kilometres. Right now, Truby seemed nothing like Ben's idea of a businessman. He was every inch the helicopter pilot – an experienced one, at that.

Ben stared out to sea. In the distance he could see the bright lights of cruise ships and freight carriers. But directly ahead, the horizon was clear.

'Have you got some sort of private island set-up?'

Truby smiled. His right hand was relaxed but steady on the cyclic. 'I think you have me confused with Richard Branson.'

'So where are we going? Bermuda?'

'Wait and see.'

Ben was secretly delighted that Addison and his mother had both agreed to sit in the luxurious passenger cabin with its leather-upholstered seats and sofa, bar and TV screens. He had Truby, the cockpit and the view all to himself. A two-way speaker system kept them in voice contact with the cabin, and Ben could hear Addison muttering to Caroline about this unexpected development.

Caroline, if she knew where they were going, was giving nothing away.

They'd flown around thirty nautical miles when Truby dropped the Sikorsky S-76 low to the water. If they'd been aboard a sea-copter, Ben would have assumed Truby was preparing to land on the waves. There was not the barest hint of any firm land.

He was itching to ask, but decided that it would look pretty uncool. His eyes rested on Truby's hands and the avionics. Ben liked machines. He'd already persuaded his parents to allow him to learn to drive a tractor, a haymaker and even his mother's Porsche Boxster around his grandfather's land near Schloss Bach. But the cockpit of Truby's helicopter was on a whole other level. There was an almost dizzying array of screens, switches and buttons. When he'd commented, Truby had only said, 'You pick it up pretty fast.'

Ben noticed that Truby's eyes kept going to a small attachment, a kind of handheld phone or device that was fixed to the helicopter's collective pitch control but, Ben now realised, might not actually be part of it.

Truby's hand went to the device he'd been eyeing. He tapped the screen in a rapid series of keystrokes. It looked like he was entering a code.

Almost immediately, the radio crackled into life. 'Arrival code received, thank you, *Gemini*. This is *Sagittarius* at One, activating landing mode. Over.'

Ben stared intently at Truby. '*Gemini*? *Sagittarius*? What are you, the Zodiac Club?'

Truby just smiled.

Before Ben could say any of the other things that were fighting for mind-space, a single blue beam of light suddenly appeared in the sky. It stood straight up out of the ocean, at least twenty metres high.

'Whoa. What the heck is *that*?'

Almost as soon as it had appeared, it was gone. But then the light appeared again, accompanied by four more blue beams of light.

'*Gemini*, prepare to land.'

The blue beams disappeared. Ben noticed that Truby had adjusted their trajectory. They were now flying straight into the centre of the area where the five lights had been.

The next time the lights appeared, they seemed to be

heating the sea water. It frothed and boiled at the source of the lights. Ben gazed, transfixed, as the water bubbled ever more violently and the blue pillars of light flashed on and off until, finally, only a single light remained.

From beneath the froth, the ocean appeared to heave and Ben could see that some kind of gigantic submersible craft was rising beneath it. He watched, his breath caught in his throat. If it was a submarine, it was an enormous vessel – as wide, at least, as an aircraft carrier and as long as a cruise liner.

'This … is … unreal.'

'It's quite real,' Truby replied. Ben didn't need to see his face to know he was smiling.

'Mum, are you seeing this?' he asked.

Over the intercom he heard Addison say, 'Damn straight we're seeing this!'

The power of speech left Ben then. There was an otherworldly quality to what was taking place before his eyes. An enormous edifice was rising up from the ocean. The entire structure was in silhouette, but it glinted very slightly when caught in the wavering beam of the chopper's searchlight.

Water fell away, collapsing in sheer waves, each around ten metres high, that crashed into the sea. A circle of lights appeared, faintly blue, like dim LEDs. They wrapped around most of the disc-like structure. Ben had a sudden impression of an airport terminal supported by four huge columns.

As its watery membrane seeped away, he could see

various features of the edifice. It looked like an oil drilling rig, crossed with a submerged spaceship. All the edges were soft, rounded as if worn smooth by the depths of the ocean. The lights were windows, Ben was almost certain: portholes behind which he caught tantalising glimpses of light.

The vertical beams of light were shining from the far end of the structure where a domed shape, some kind of roof, was rolling to one side, revealing a platform. The moment the platform was clear of the water, the vertical beams blinked out.

'Switching to guide LEDs, *Gemini*. Over.'

A row of dimly lit green discs, each no more than the size of a tennis ball, appeared ahead of them. Eerily suspended, apparently in the middle of the sky, Ben realised that the lights delineated the upper edge of the platform.

'Is this some kind of secret airport?'

Truby didn't answer. 'Switching chopper to dark mode, One. Over.'

The rising platform had come to a halt. It had risen more than thirty metres, and now towered over the helicopter. Ben guessed that there was still more of it beneath the water, maybe a lot more. The helicopter began to swoop upwards, aiming for the top of the platform. As they cleared the row of lights around the edge of the risen platform, Ben noticed that they immediately turned off. The sky and sea were dark. The enormous black shadow beneath them felt suddenly ominous – a giant, placid sea monster, waiting silently to swallow them whole.

'Turning landing LEDs on, *Gemini*.'

'Roger that, One.'

A rectangle of orange lights appeared below them now. They were so faint that Ben could hardly make them out, but Truby seemed better attuned. Within a minute he'd positioned the helicopter directly above the centre of the rectangle. Now they were hovering.

'You're cleared to land, *Gemini*.'

Ben thought he detected a faint German accent in the voice of *Sagittarius*.

They began to drop vertically.

This was Ben's favourite part of riding in a helicopter. The last time he'd been in one, they'd been searching for a glimpse of his father somewhere under the Annapurna region of the Himalayan mountains. The memory was momentarily painful, but the experience of being inside an aircraft that was descending into a mysterious *something* was distracting.

As they dropped, Ben realised that the gigantic platform was falling, too – sinking back into the ocean with the helicopter and the four of them inside.

Jonah into the whale.

Nobody inside the helicopter so much as breathed a syllable.

Above the clatter of the rotor blades, Ben heard the grinding mechanism of the roof rolling back into place overhead. For a few seconds, Truby's features were bathed only in the dappled rainbow of lights from the avionics.

And then the bay around them erupted with light.

The entire wall to Truby's right began to slide into the floor. Beyond, Ben saw a sight that was possibly the last thing he could have expected – a vast open space that was clearly a combination of functional offices and living quarters – distinct areas decorated in kookily uncoordinated fashion.

It was like stumbling into the underwater offices of some achingly trendy dotcom.

Breathless, Ben turned to Truby. 'You've got to be kidding. Trubycom has headquarters under the sea?'

'No joke, Ben.' Truby grinned and gestured at the base with his hand. 'This is not Trubycom. Caroline, Addison, Ben; welcome to Gemini Force One.'

GEMINI FORCE ONE

'I hate to be a wise guy, but I'm gonna remind you that you all signed a confidentiality agreement,' Truby shouted over the sound of the decelerating helicopter blades. The clatter echoed around the walls of the hangar bay into which Truby had lowered the Sikorsky S-76.

Ben blinked. Slowly, he climbed out of the helicopter after Caroline and Addison. He stood gawping at the view of this underwater base that Truby had referred to as Gemini Force One.

'What is this place?' Ben asked.

Truby grinned and straightened up a little. 'Gemini Force is my new – and completely secret – project. We're a rescue agency at heart. But I like to think we have a few pretty special features. This is our base and the most important of all the craft we have here: Gemini Force One.'

They were gazing out at a circular chamber that was attached to the helo-deck. Windows wrapped around the entire structure. Some seemed to be opaque; others showed the sea beyond – moving dark water in which shadows stirred.

Ben could see two levels of the main deck. They'd descended to the lower level as the helo-deck had dropped. Now he saw that a mezzanine level was connected by a swirl of steps at two ends. Both levels were centred on an inner circular chamber. Whatever was inside the chamber didn't seem too covert, however, as there were several open doors. From where Ben stood, it looked pretty much like a fancy conference room: screens on the walls and a round table with a high-backed chair at every position.

Beyond that was what looked like the command centre. Two young men stood before an array of nine high-definition screens. Ben guessed they were roughly the same age as Addison – mid-twenties. They were chatting quietly, and didn't even seem to have noticed the arrival of Truby's helicopter. But, of course, they must have done.

Ben's guess? *Too cool for school.*

A tall Asian man, no older than thirty, stood about five metres away from them. He wore metallic-sheened, anthracite-coloured salopettes with a charcoal-grey T-shirt. In one hand was a steaming mug. He was regarding the visitors with mild curiosity, both shoulder straps hanging loosely from his waist. Combined with the man's dark eyes, angular cheekbones, tousled black hair and casual stance, it gave him a certain charm.

Next to Ben, Addison grinned widely at him and waved. 'Hey.'

The guy seemed a little surprised by the gesture. He glanced at Truby as if for guidance.

'Toru, these are the people I've been telling you

about. Addison Nicole Dyer, Caroline and Ben Carrington, meet Toru Takitani. He's our lead pilot. Used to be a flyboy with the Japanese Self-Defense Force. Toru, Addison's crazier'n you, from what I've seen. Saw her jump out of an Aermacchi, zip through the air and snatch a parachutist clean out of a one-way ride to oblivion.'

With a slow formality, Toru bowed his head.

'Flyboy?' Addison said with a smile.

The corner of his mouth twitched in what might have been disdain. When he spoke it was with a languid, West Coast-inflected Japanese accent. 'That's the kind of respect we get around here. You'll be "flygirl".'

'S'all right by me.'

Ben shook Toru's hand. 'You're a pilot?'

'About half of Gemini Force are pilots,' Toru replied.

Ben was only slowly adjusting to the reality of Gemini Force. 'Sorry, hang on, are you saying you fly other things out of here – apart from the Sikorsky?'

Truby said, 'You can't see them from here, but we have a bunch of aircraft pods attached around the base.'

'Aircraft pods,' Ben pronounced. 'You take off … from here?'

'Gemini Force One is fifty-four nautical miles from the western tip of the island of Cozumel. At that distance, our activity, so long as it doesn't contravene maritime law, isn't subject to the laws of any country.' Truby grinned. 'Makes my life a hell of a lot easier. No planning permission, so long as I don't fish or drill for oil. Makes me want to shift my entire Trubycom operation onto a floating platform, if you want the truth.'

Ben was lost in wonder. It took him a couple of seconds to order his ideas. Then he began to shoot questions. 'Where do you get your power?'

Truby hesitated very slightly before answering, 'It's nuclear.'

'How many planes?'

'We prefer "vehicles". Air – four including the Sikorsky. Sea and ground – a few more.'

'How much did all this cost?'

'Trubycom does OK, son.'

'You may have the wealth of Croesus,' observed Caroline rather dryly – her first comment. 'But this venture won't make you any richer.'

Ruefully, Truby nodded. 'I'll take that.'

Ben continued, 'And you're miles from *every*where. What kind of rescues are you going to carry out?'

'There's no perfect location, Ben. I chose this place for its proximity to hurricane areas and the United States.'

Addison said, 'Patriotism?'

Truby shrugged. 'If you like.'

Addison draped one arm round Ben's shoulder. She turned to Truby. 'Y'all got a pretty amazing place here. How in heck d'you keep it a secret?'

Truby and Toru exchanged a barely perceptible glance, but Ben noticed that they didn't answer her question.

Caroline stood in graceful silence, taking in her surroundings.

Truby turned to her. 'You've not said too much, Ceecee. Can I get you a coffee? We have a Nespresso station just around here. Or maybe you're ready to take the tour?'

It struck Ben that Truby was trying to impress his mother. It wasn't the first time he'd had the feeling and he wasn't sure how to react. Old blokes hitting on your mum wasn't cool. But somehow, when it was Jason Truby, it didn't seem quite so gross. If it wasn't for the fact that his father had died so recently, Ben might even have been glad to see his mother hook up with a man like Truby.

Yes, he thought. *Truby might just be worthy of Countess Caroline Brandis-Carrington.*

◣ BEN ◢

'If it's all right with you,' Truby said, addressing Ben and Addison, 'I'd like to talk privately with the countess.'

Ben shrugged. There was plenty to see. 'Sure. Can we take a look downstairs?'

Truby nodded, so Ben and Addison headed off together.

The helo-deck was on a mezzanine level off Gemini Force One's main deck. A staircase led down to a second level which contained the sleeping quarters, a hospital and a gym.

The flanks of the circular space were zoned for living quarters. There was just enough room for four double cabins on either side of the deck. A central space adjacent to the windows on the east-facing side of the deck was dominated by a living room. Its decor seemed at odds with much of the modernity of the base: a living space in shabby antique chic.

Next to him Ben heard Addison chuckle under her breath. 'OK, sure, whatever.'

He whispered, 'What's up?'

'Isn't this just what you'd expect from some ageing California hippy made good in Silicon Valley?'

In one corner of the living area the floor was panelled

with strips of maple wood. There were chintzy sofas. Antique wooden chairs painted white or pastel blue were arranged around coffee tables, with a couple of vintage floor lamps. It looked like furniture shops Ben had seen on the King's Road in Chelsea. A minute or two after Ben and Addison arrived on the second deck they were joined by two more members of Gemini Force – the guys Ben had spotted upstairs, playing it cool. Now, it was all smiles and introductions.

'Hi, I'm Paul Scott!' A tall, sandy-haired guy with a thick, floppy fringe shook first Ben's and then Addison's hand. His accent immediately invoked Australia. 'Is that your mother upstairs, with Truby? Impressive lady! I bet she's being given the hard sell right about now. He's taken her into the conference room. Bit of an honour, that.'

'I should warn you about Paul,' broke in the second guy. He was a little shorter than Paul, with heavier, more muscular shoulders visible beneath the tight fabric of his grey T-shirt. From his accent and demeanour, Ben could tell immediately that he was from Scotland. 'The Aussie has a strange sense of humour.' He shook Addison's hand, almost entirely ignoring Ben. 'I'm Tim Hardy. It's very nice to meet you. I hear you're think-ing of joining us. Please say yes.' Tim finished his little speech with an easy grin.

'So, Tim and Paul,' Ben said. They gave him a quick, almost cursory nod, and returned their attentions to Addison.

'We saw that thing you did in Abu Dhabi,' Paul said.

'Yeah, that was incredible. How did you know you'd be able to catch your mate?' Tim asked.

'I trained with the paras in Western Australia for six months,' Paul said. 'And I still don't think I'd have been able to do what you did.'

'Did you know you had totally *mental* skills when you jumped?' Tim added with a cheeky smile.

They stopped, waiting for her to reply. Addison merely widened her eyes at Ben. 'Who's been talking?'

Ben acknowledged her glance with a quick grin. He couldn't help but feel a stab of pride that his mother had picked this amazing woman to be her partner in the Caroliners. These Gemini Force pilots had turned into total fanboys around her. Thanks to Addison and Caroline, he was now getting to see something as fully awesome as Gemini Force One. All he wanted to do right now was see the rest of the base, understand how the team worked, find out what planes they flew, how they'd got started in this life.

Meanwhile, it was clear that Paul and Tim just wanted to flirt with Addison.

At least Toru wasn't joining in. He stood patiently by, arms crossed over his chest, a half-smile on his face as he watched his fellow pilots.

'Don't mind Tim and Paul,' Toru commented, catching Ben's eye. 'They get like this. When they can, that is. Julia just blanks them.'

'Julia?'

'Julia Bencke. She's an aeronautical engineer,' Toru said, 'and a damn good helicopter pilot. One tough Brazilian lady.'

'Take no notice of Captain Takitani here,' Paul advised. 'He doesn't like to see us having fun.'

'Well, that's kind of inappropriate in a professional setting,' Addison growled.

The two pilots turned to her with expressions of dismay. 'What, having fun?'

'Yeah, what happens around here when you get serious? *Can* you get serious?'

Tim and Paul stared at each other in obvious bewilderment. After a second, Addison broke into wreaths of smiles. 'Man, but you boys are *ea-sy*! Damn, it's gonna be a lot of fun yanking your chains.'

Ben had had enough of the banter. He wanted to get a proper look around. 'So, guys, where are the aircraft? And where are all the other staff?'

It seemed that only Toru was willing to help out. 'When we're fully operational, we're going to have a skeleton staff of five at all times: one medic, two pilots, one operations guy, one mechanic. But today it's just me and these two nimrods.'

'What about the planes?'

Tim frowned. 'You don't want to bother with the flyboy stuff, Ben. You should see my little baby, *Pisces*. Thing of beauty. Top speed of thirty-five knots. As happy on the surface as underwater. Seats eighty people in comfort.'

Paul grinned. 'Not exactly *comfort*.'

'They'll be grateful to squeeze aboard,' Tim said. 'You wait and see.'

'How about you, Paul? What do you pilot?' Ben asked, fascinated.

'I'm kind of a backup pilot – I can fly any of our craft. But mainly I concentrate on ground vehicles – diggers, drilling machinery, that kind of thing.'

'And you, Toru?'

Paul replied quickly, 'He flies GF Two and his mission call sign is *Leo*. All the vehicles have numbers. The base, of course, is GF One. The other vehicles are GF Two, GF Three – well, you get the gist! But the numbers get kind of boring, so we started calling the craft after their pilots. That's why you'll usually hear GF Two referred to as *Leo* – Toru's call sign – and GF Five referred to as *Pisces,* Tim's call sign. And so on. During missions, I'm *Capricorn*. Whatever I'm driving hitches a ride with *Leo*. And *Leo* goes anywhere, fast.'

Ben turned to Toru. '*Leo* is the biggest of the lot?'

'It's not as big as *Pisces* but, fully loaded, it's almost as heavy. And *Leo* can transport other vehicles – such as GF Three, *Scorpio*,' Toru replied.

'But *Leo* is the most expensive piece of kit?'

The three pilots shared a glance. Tim blew a low whistle, shaking his head. 'Och, no. Don't you believe it.'

Paul said, 'She's only small. But she's the diva of the team, definitely.'

'She?'

'GF Four, also known as *Aquarius*. There's no aircraft like her – in the *world*.'

The group fell silent as they were joined by Truby and Caroline. Ben watched his mother being introduced to Tim and Paul. In Caroline's presence, both men became reflective and respectful, exchanging pleasantries about where they were from (Aberdeen and Perth – 'But not the Scottish one,' Paul told her, with a smile).

Truby had asked Caroline for time alone, presumably to make what Ben hoped was the offer to join forces at which he'd hintèd back in St Anton. The two had talked privately for less than ten minutes – Ben hoped that was because his mother had found the decision easy to make. His own mind was already made up.

What was left for his mother back in Austria? Renovating a crumbling stately home? There were so many better ways for her to spend her time. A stroke of intense good fortune had brought Caroline, Addison and Truby together. Ben felt it had to be for a reason.

'So – good talk?' Ben asked.

Unhelpfully, Caroline merely gave him a vague, smiling nod.

Ben sighed. He'd have to be more direct. 'Mum. Seriously, now. This place is amazing. Let me work here and I'll forget all about the army.'

Truby chuckled. 'Don't get ahead of yourself, kiddo. Don't you have school?'

A shard of disappointment stabbed at him, but Ben was determined not to show it. 'Yeah, course, school, for now. I'm just saying that, Mum … you and Addi. You should join.' He turned to Truby. 'I mean, that's what you want, right? Addi and Mum, in Gemini Force? That's why you brought us here?'

Truby nodded. 'Yes. I already talked to your mom about that. Addison, what do you say? Your skydive above the Sky-High works as an audition piece, for me. We'd love to have you on the crew.'

Addison cast her eyes around the lower deck and gave a casual shrug, as though he'd asked her if she wanted thousand-island or blue-cheese dressing on her salad. She nodded. 'OK. Sure. Sounds like a blast.'

'You're certain? Don't you want to see the aircraft first?' Truby asked.

'Is it better'n that Aermacchi?'

Truby couldn't suppress a grin. 'Hell, yeah!'

'Then I'm in.'

'How about you, Countess?'

There was a considered pause. 'Let's take things slowly,' Caroline said, artfully. 'I'll stay for a month. And then we'll see.'

Ben clenched a fist and slowly pulled it to his chest. His lips moved to form a silent, resounding, 'Yeesss!'

⟶ TRUBY CENTRAL ⟵

'Party time,' Tim had told Ben with a wink, as they'd piled on board the Sikorsky S-76 with Truby, Addison and Ben's mother. 'We're off to Truby Central.'

The helicopter had landed in the front garden of Truby's villa on the east coast of the island of Cozumel. It had occurred to Ben that Truby had deliberately picked an isolated spot. On this coast there was precious little but nature. The beaches were too wild, the sea too unpredictable. The entire island population was clustered around the sheltered western coast. They'd turned their backs to the open ocean.

This was hurricane country.

Now, Ben sipped his Coke and watched Truby, who had made shrimp *ceviche* and was offering it around in small ceramic bowls, all neatly hand-painted in distinct, multicoloured designs. A wood-fired barbecue smouldered in one corner of the patio just outside the lounge area where most of the guests were standing with glasses in their hands. A member of Truby's household staff, a young man, was seasoning steaks, chicken breasts and salmon fillets in the open-plan kitchen.

Caroline and Addison joined Ben at the window. The moon had risen. Almost full, it lit a section of black sea like a searchlight. For a moment they all stood quietly, enjoying the view of silhouetted palm trees bending in the wind.

'You were very quick to accept Jason's offer,' Caroline said to Addison.

When Addison didn't reply, Ben prompted teasingly, 'Maybe Addi likes what she sees.'

Sharply, Addison turned to him. 'It wasn't that.'

With a friendly smile he said, 'I'm just really pleased you accepted.'

Caroline agreed. 'We're big fans of yours, you know.'

Addison said, 'And what about you, Ceecee? You decided yet?'

'Ben's desperate for me to get involved. Well, you can see that for yourself.'

'But he's right – and so is Truby,' Addison said. 'You'd be good for Gemini Force.'

Ben grinned broadly. 'There you go, Mum. What she said!'

Caroline's smile seemed suddenly filled with sadness.

'Ceecee – you're not feeling it?' Addison sounded concerned.

'I do "feel it". But I also feel quite badly out of my depth.'

Ben said, 'It *would* be a lot to learn but, Mum, you'd enjoy that.'

'There's still rather a lot to do with Carrington International. They're prosecuting some of the directors. I'll probably have to appear as a witness,' Caroline sighed.

'Heck, Ceecee. That's rough,' Addison replied.

'You can see why Gemini Force rather has its appeal.'

'But you've got doubts?'

'I have. And, just between the three of us, I'm a little nervous.'

'Mum – seriously? You rock!' Ben told her, moving away to where Truby was showing off his sound system to Tim. Within seconds, Ben had managed to persuade them to plug his own MP3 player into the amplifier and play the latest album by Rock Snakes of Mars. Tim began to chat enthusiastically about the group. According to him they were 'totally sick'.

Chatting to the young pilot was pretty cool. Ben was eager for the chance to talk to everyone in Gemini Force, but especially the pilots. Most of the crew had stayed behind on Gemini Force One, but Truby had promised that Julia Bencke and Lola Reyes, the junior medic, would be joining them later at the villa.

'We don't socialise too much at GF One,' Tim had said. 'We save that for Truby Central – Jason's villa.'

The air began to shudder with the sound of a second helicopter. It was flying in from the east. As it flew over the house, the windows trembled. Truby strolled over to stand beside Ben.

'Impact-resistant glass,' he said. 'It's laminated. The whole house is set up to withstand a hurricane. It's the only way to feel safe, especially on this side of the island.'

'Why didn't you just buy a house on the other side, the one with all the great beaches?' Ben asked.

'Great beaches – and *all the other people*,' Truby replied pointedly.

'Fair enough. You're going for peace and quiet?'

Truby considered this. 'I'm going for *quiet*.'

Ben nodded, thoughtfully. 'Makes sense.'

Through the window they watched a second Sikorsky S-76 landing on the generous front lawn, a space as large as two basketball courts and covered in the kind of glassy scrub grass that you got on Caribbean golf courts. Like the chopper in which they'd flown with Truby, it was painted white with narrow stripes in powder blue along its flank. There were no distinctive markings – it was an out-of-the-box craft.

Addison sidled up behind Ben. 'Check it out,' she whispered. 'No markings.'

Ben answered without turning around. 'Truby doesn't want people recognising him. He's on this side of the island so that he doesn't attract attention. Gemini Force is a secret. I tried using my phone to look it up on the internet when we got to the villa. Nothing.'

Silently, Addison mouthed, 'Ask yourself – why?'

It was a good question. Was real secrecy even possible? Ben couldn't help thinking that the instant one of the Gemini Force aircraft turned up on a rescue mission, the world would start talking.

On Gemini Force One, Toru had shown him his flight jacket, part of a muted uniform that consisted of Scarpa boots, cargo-pant-style salopettes made from woven Kevlar fibres and plain T-shirts. The jacket was anthracite-coloured Kevlar, fitted and down-filled, decorated only with an embroidered logo in red, white and blue: Gemini Force and the number of each member's vehicle. Most team members would wear the Gemini Force One badge, Toru had told Ben – that was all the operational staff, the medics and, of course, Truby himself, as they all worked on the main base. Only the pilots wore badges for the other vehicles. In Toru's case, it was the badge for Gemini Force Two.

Those badges are going to provoke questions, Ben thought. *Questions like, 'Who is behind Gemini Force?'*

Two young women were jogging towards the villa, heads lowered as the helicopter blades whirred to a halt over them. One woman was white with hair the colour of dark honey; the other woman was black with light brown, straight hair. As they came closer, Ben realised that the black woman was young – maybe only twenty years old. The fair-haired woman looked older – around thirty. She was the first to introduce herself.

'Hey, Tim. Hello Addison, Benedict. I'm Julia Bencke.'

Julia's English was perfect but Ben could detect a faint accent. He remembered that she'd been described as a 'tough Brazilian lady'.

The younger woman brushed a long lock of fine brown hair from her face. Shyly, she smiled at Addison, and then Ben. She was slim with a flawless, cinnamon-coloured complexion and grey eyes. Ben's attention locked onto her immediately.

Before she could speak, Truby said, 'Everyone, meet

Julia Bencke and Lola Reyes. Julia's a former engineer at Embraer in Brazil – she's our main chopper pilot. Lola's from Miami. She's on our medical team. Lola just finished top of her year at Harvard Med.'

'Harvard Med, wow,' Ben said, unable to prevent a wistful sigh from entering his voice. 'You must be, like, completely brilliant.'

OK, so she's probably a bit older than twenty, he thought privately. *More like twenty-three, twenty-four? Is that too old for me? So what? I look older than sixteen – and Lola's cute.*

'The whole *team* is brilliant,' Truby said, a steely note in his voice. 'Every last one of them. That's why I wanted them for Gemini Force.'

Ben couldn't help feeling more than a little crestfallen. All this talent, all these amazing people, that incredible underwater base. And yet, tomorrow he had to return to England and Kenton College.

What a waste!

KENTON COLLEGE

The 'beak' was waiting for him next to the lacrosse pitch. When Ben had heard he'd be getting Lawrence Sandwell as his form tutor for sixth form, he'd practically begged his parents to remove him.

Sandwell loathed Ben.

The college regularly came in the top three schools in the UK league tables of exam results. Fees had become so high that parents expected a guaranteed place at Oxbridge or Imperial College. The pressure on school places was tougher now that the wealthy folk of China and Russia had decided that a British public school was the best route to Oxbridge or the Ivy League.

The boys who'd scraped through the Common Entrance exam didn't impress Sandwell. He disliked many of the sporty but non-academic boys. As head of Sixth, he made a point of getting most of them to transfer to another school before they reached sixth form and impacted on the school's coveted A-level league table position.

Ben had so far resisted these efforts. When he was thirteen, he'd achieved one of the best results in Common Entrance. Since starting at Kenton, however, his academic achievements had become totally overshadowed. Being captain of lacrosse and a star of the football and orient-eering teams didn't leave much spare time for study.

His GCSE results had been good enough to keep Ben in the sixth form – just about. But Sandwell had it in for him. It was personal. There was definitely a whiff of envy. Ben had experienced it elsewhere – people imply-ing that he was only at Kenton because of his rich father. He didn't dare to reply with his actual entrance exam score. It just made them angrier. The only way was to prove himself worthy by being better than everyone else.

Somewhere along the line, that had come to mean excelling on the sports fields. Ben had kept telling him-self that as far as exams went, he'd be able to catch up. He'd never admitted it to anyone, but his GCSEs had come as a horrible shock. Suddenly a couple of nights' revision was only enough to get him B grades and the occasional A.

Sandwell was clever enough to keep his miserly graces within the bounds of acceptable teacher behaviour. He focused everything on Ben's academic performance. Definitely Ben's weakest point.

That morning when he sidled up to Ben, Sandwell had mischief in mind.

Ben was nursing a bruise he'd been given just above the knee. It was going to hurt for days. When he looked up, there was his least favourite 'beak' – the boys' slang term for the teachers.

'Carrington. I imagine you're relieved to be back on

the pitch?' Sandwell's obsequious smile was as sickening as ever. 'Rotten summer you must have had.'

Ben straightened up and leaned his lacrosse stick against the nearby wall. 'It wasn't great,' he conceded. If he could have talked about Gemini Force and Jason Truby, he might have been able to tell Sandwell that as grimly as the summer had started, it had ended on a note of sheer exhilaration.

'No. I'm sorry about that, of course. But Carrington Junior, lad, we need, you and I, to have a somewhat serious discussion of your progress. Academically speaking. Your father isn't around to mould you into some semblance of a candidate for the Russell Group,' he said with a forced chuckle. 'May he rest in peace. But I'm sure he still wants it done.'

'I don't want to go to a Russell Group university,' Ben said.

'When the Bank of Dad pays the fees, we all have to do as we're told.'

Ben glared. 'It's the Bank of Mum now,' he said, softly.

The smirk that appeared on Sandwell's face at that moment was worthy of a fist. Ben felt a surge of rage colour his cheeks. Still his form tutor smiled, one arm held straight out, shepherding Ben away from the pitch.

How am I supposed to put up with this for another ten months? Ben wondered.

'I think it's time we had a talk,' Sandwell said. 'Shall we say in ten minutes, my office?'

As soon as Sandwell bid him a temporary farewell

at the door to the changing room, Ben reached for his mobile phone. Just as he had done at least twenty times a day since leaving Gemini Force One, he checked for a message from Lola Reyes. When he didn't see one he tapped out a text to her: *Just got hassled by the biggest jerk in school. That's my afternoon ruined. How's you? Just another sunny day on GF1?*

After a few moments, resigned to the fact that Lola probably wasn't going to answer the text right away, Ben changed out of his lacrosse kit and into casual clothes. He'd done all his prep and his one requisite daily extra-curricular activity – the rest of the day was his. Unfortunately, Sandwell was planning to suck the life out of him for longer than would be tolerable.

As he walked, painstakingly slowly, to Sandwell's office in the main school building, Ben wondered what Lola and the others would be doing right now. It was morning in the Caribbean. They'd probably be eating poached eggs and fruit in the casual dining area on the lower floor. Sunlight would be streaming through the surface of the sea, a brilliant turquoise band around the base. The crew would probably be enjoying their breakfast while shoals of shiny yellow and silver fish fluttered around the windows of Gemini Force One.

His mother would probably be getting to know how everything worked on the base. Or maybe she'd be working out in the gym area, or teaching the others something about climbing. His mother did know an astonishing amount about knots, it had to be said.

He arrived at Sandwell's office.

Behind the door, Ben was slightly unnerved by the cold expression in Sandwell's eyes now – as though his previous friendly demeanour had been entirely for show.

'Carrington, this won't take long. I've discussed it with the head and also with your house master. They agree with me that if you're to improve your grades enough to avoid thoroughly disgracing Kenton College, then the lacrosse will have to stop. And the football. And the orienteering.'

Ben gaped. 'They're the only things that make my life worth living!'

Sandwell twisted his features into a tragi-comic frown. 'Alas! Perhaps you'll find hitherto unexpected pleasures in the quietude of our library and in the intellectual companionship of your fellow scholars? Because, Carrington, I'd say that aptly summarises your future at Kenton.'

Inwardly, Ben sighed. It was going to be a long few weeks.

⟣ FAMILIE DIETZ ⟢

The weeks passed. Ben avoided the newspapers, especially the finance pages, for which the demise of Carrington International was a soap opera. He kept his head down and studied.

His current grades were averaging around a high B, but then he'd had a lot to catch up with. A or even A★ grades were likely if he kept up this level of intensity. The head himself had promised Ben that he could return to all the sporting teams when he achieved AAB – the grades needed to access most of Britain's top universities.

Sandwell probably thought he'd got through to him, but Ben hated studying so hard. All that sustained him was the thought of half term and a return to Gemini Force One.

Six weeks later, the day arrived. Ben headed straight for Heathrow Airport and boarded a plane for Cancun International, where Truby himself picked him up in a Sikorsky S-76.

'We've made some changes since you were last here.'

There was no denying the glint in Truby's eye. Ben could barely remain in his seat.

Before his first visit to Gemini Force One, Ben had

felt fairly confident that he'd seen most of the seriously cool things that awaited anyone on the planet. Being the son of Casper Carrington, he'd travelled to sixteen different countries, eaten in the world's best restaurants, skied from helicopters and been chauffeured around in fast cars and private jets. Ben knew it had been an incredibly privileged existence. He also realised that it had made him annoyingly difficult to impress.

Ben was still relishing the fact that there were, after all, wonders in the world that could blow his mind. The awe he'd experienced walking around Gemini Force One had penetrated his soul. It was the first thing in his mind when he woke up and his last thought before falling asleep.

He'd never been in love, but he could only imagine that it felt something like this. He wondered if his mother felt the same way.

Caroline Brandis-Carrington always needed a mission in life. Now her husband was dead. His business was in ruins and his fortune gone. Even her own new venture had been demolished in the fallout. Truby's offer to buy the Caroliners and roll them into Gemini Force would save Caroline Brandis-Carrington, Ben was convinced of that.

Ben asked, 'What kind of changes?'

'Well ... your mother approves.'

'Oh, I get it. "Wait and see"?'

'Bingo, kid.'

Truby had spent the first ten minutes of the flight

pointing out various features of the helicopter's controls. Now Ben shifted, impatient. His gaze landed on the speed gauge. He checked the milometer. Something didn't make sense.

'Did we take a different route?'

'Nope.'

'Huh. I must have remembered it wrong. Isn't GF One fifty-four nautical miles from your house on Cozumel?'

'Fifty-four point four.'

'So shouldn't we be able to see the base? I'm pretty sure we could see the lights when we were this close, last time.'

There was a hint of teasing in Truby's words. 'Last time? Maybe so. But that was *then*.'

The helicopter began to drop. In the sky ahead, something flickered into view. Ben was very still, staring intently. There was definitely *something* hovering above the waves, appearing within an elliptical shape about fifty metres ahead.

'What *is* that?'

A voice came over the radio then, giving Truby landing instructions. A new voice, not one that Ben recognised. Then he heard, unmistakeable, his mother's voice.

'Ben, darling, I can't wait to see you.'

The S-76 slowed and began to sink gently as if it were coming in to land. Ben stared straight down. The evidence of his own eyes was undeniable – directly below them was Gemini Force One, in 'regular landing mode'.

For the first time, he was seeing the base by natural light. In broad daylight it wasn't quite the dramatic, looming, floodlit presence that he'd encountered that first night. Only the helicopter landing pod was exposed above the ocean, but through clear, aquamarine water Ben could see the rest of the base. It was a mottled collection of russets, forest greens and coral pinks. It didn't look like a reef *exactly*, not to an educated eye, but to someone throwing a glance down as they flew high overhead, Ben could see that it would be convincing.

'Wait … where'd that come from? How did we not see it before? Have you got some new way to make the base pop up really fast?'

'I've got a new way of tricking the eye,' Truby replied.

'Like what – mirrors?'

Truby lowered the S-76 into the open pod below. 'Like, bending light,' he said. There was wonder in his voice.

When the doors to the helipad rolled back to cover the ceiling, Ben's mother was standing there to meet him, together with Tim, Paul and another two people that Ben hadn't met before.

One was a man in his forties, about five feet, ten inches tall with short, yet unruly, fair hair that was greying all over. He had calm hazel eyes and was dressed in the full Gemini Force uniform. He immediately began talking intently with Truby. Next to him, in denim shorts, flip-flops and a powder-blue T-shirt, was a petite, friendly-looking girl with long, light brown hair. She looked to be roughly the same age as Ben. She was giving him a knowing grin.

Tim greeted Ben with a matey fist and shoulder bump. Ever since they'd chatted at Truby's villa, Ben felt that Tim was the male pilot with whom he'd possibly have the most rapport, which slightly surprised him. He'd have expected to bond most with the ex-military members of Gemini Force, but maybe Tim was just the most naturally amiable person on the base.

Toru, a few metres away in the central lounge area, managed a wave. All the while, Ben tried to keep his eyes from roving around, searching out the junior medic, Lola Reyes.

Ben was enjoying how the teenage girl kept looking at him, waiting to be introduced. But after the friendly texts he'd exchanged with Lola while he was at school, it was still a teeny bit disappointing that she hadn't turned out to say hello. Maybe he'd read too much into her texts? She'd kept them pretty vague, just the occasional smiley and 'Ha ha' to his jokes.

Finally, Truby seemed to finish talking to the forty-something guy about whatever it was that was so engrossing and turned back to Ben.

'Meet Michael Dietz and his daughter, Jasmine. They're the other resident family on GF One. Dietz is part of the crew. He's kind of my right-hand man here.

Jasmine lives in Geneva. Like you, she'll be visiting us during vacations.'

Ben greeted Jasmine with the practised enthusiasm he used with girls at parties in London. 'Hi, I'm Benedict,' he said, flashing a grin. Then he prayed she'd start talking first. If not, they were sunk. Girls his own age kind of scared him. After the introductory bits, Ben didn't really know how to do conversation. His 'banter' would usually falter after a few minutes. Topics would come to mind one after the other, only to be rejected before he'd voiced them.

What did girls even like? They didn't seem to get enthused when he told them what he'd read about the latest version of *Call of Duty*. Statistics about the size and construction of the latest skyscraper left them cold. Their Facebook updates often puzzled him.

Ben would be expected to get on with Jasmine Dietz – he could see that right away. She was certainly pretty, with her wavy, long brown hair and a very sweet-featured, heart-shaped face. The adults were already pulling away, with an air of having important work to do. Ben and Jasmine were left beaming at each other in awkward but hopeful silence.

'Did they put the invisibility on?' Jasmine had a soft German inflection to her Americanised English. Ben guessed that she was probably at one of the international schools in Geneva. He was relieved that she'd chosen to address him in English. Ben's German was fluent but clunky, only ever used in German lessons, with his grandfather and in the village of Bach.

'Indeed they did! And it was pretty, pretty, *pretty* cool.'

She frowned, rather sweet in her concentration. 'Really? From what I hear, it's imperfect. Most of the visible light can bend around the base, but not all of it. You're lucky! I haven't seen it yet. My dad only finished testing it today.'

'Bending light, huh? I'm going to have to Google that. I don't think A-level physics quite covers it.'

Jasmine laughed. 'Truby always believed it would work. He funded my dad's work when no one else would. Dad practically worships him.'

Ben smiled. 'You know what, I don't normally go in for hero worship but I have to say that everything I'm seeing at GF One is sort of pushing the limits on that.'

Jasmine raised an eyebrow. 'If you feel that way now … then what I'm about to show you may just push you over the edge.'

⟞ MARINA ⟝

Jasmine gave Ben a quick grin. She turned and began to walk, fast; down the stairs and across the second deck, beneath the helo-deck and through a corridor. On one side was the medical unit, on the other a well-equipped gym. As they sped past curved walls and windows, Ben caught a glimpse of Lola Reyes at a computer. She didn't even see him – her attention was completely absorbed by whatever she was looking at on-screen.

Beside some closed, sliding doors, Jasmine paused. It looked like a lift, with two buttons on the wall to the right. Ben didn't remember seeing any of this by the medical area when he'd first visited. The area had been covered with tarpaulin then, still being decorated. Or so he'd assumed.

Jasmine touched a button. The doors opened. Ben found himself staring right into the lift, but its three other walls only reached to his waist. The rest was open to the chamber beyond – a space filled with brilliant greens, muted turquoise-blue light and the dazzling white churn of a ten-metre waterfall. It was like stumbling across an ideal jungle picnic spot. The whole area was circled with palm trees and creepers as water tumbled into a crystal-clear plunge pool of deep aquamarine.

Jasmine took Ben's hand, a gentle smile on her lips. She stepped inside the lift.

'Truby calls this ... the Marina room,' she told Ben as the lift started downwards.

A roar of tumbling water filled the air. Light streamed in through a ceiling striped with sections of thick glass. Ben could see that the ceiling was probably less than twenty metres below the surface of the ocean.

The lift stopped, the doors opened and Jasmine led Ben over to the plunge pool. Perched at the edge, Ben turned, slowly taking in the view. The pool was several metres across. Its surface was still at the edges but churned white where the falling water sluiced in.

Opposite the waterfall, instead of the smooth interior walls of the base, there were sheer rock faces – realistic yet artificial climbing walls. Every now and then a rope hung from the ceiling, about seven metres above the highest point of the waterfall. Behind the waterfall, Ben saw that part of the exterior wall was thick glass – a window to the ocean depths. Palm fronds, rainforest ferns and hibiscus flowers in flamboyant reds and pinks filled the rest of the space.

'Sea water is piped in from the top, cascades down and gets recycled out the other end,' Jasmine told Ben. 'The hydroelectric power it generates is used to air-condition the whole room.'

'One of my dad's hotels has a lobby something like

this,' Ben said. 'Palm trees, waterfalls, a pool, rattan chairs. The whole bit.'

'But was it under water?'

They shared a grin. 'Obviously this is *way* better,' Ben confessed. 'So, this light-bending technology. Can you explain how it works?'

'My dad built it – so it's better if you ask him. It's a light shield.'

'A *shield*?'

'More like a cloaking device. You know – something like in *Star Trek*? On GF One they have this cylinder of invisibility, some new technology. The Pentagon has been researching it for years. You know the Pentagon, in the USA?'

'The Department of Defense has invisibility tech? Yikes. I can see that causing some problems. Hardly going to make America any more popular among the rest of the world powers, is it?'

Jasmine continued, 'Trubycom supplied some of the key components, so Jason gets to try it out. It doesn't work for soldiers yet, because it's not two-way. Inside the cylinder, you can't see out.'

'But it might work to disguise installations, temporarily?'

She nodded. 'Exactly.'

Invisibility.

'Sweet. I can see why it makes sense to use it on GF One – the base is only exposed temporarily. What about power?'

'We're nuclear-powered, so there's no shortage of electricity. They're going to use the shield every time the base rises out of the ocean. Anyone on a plane will still be able to catch a glimpse, if they look quickly. You may have noticed – the whole base is painted to look like a reef. It's not convincing if you look really hard. But for a quick glance, it does the job.'

Ben nodded, thinking through the implications of Gemini Force One's situation in the Caribbean Sea. 'But it means that passing yachts and ships, if they stray from the shipping lanes, I guess they shouldn't see too much.'

'Yes and, anyway, the base is built on some kind of sweet spot between lanes. Big ships shouldn't get anywhere close.'

'What about yachts?'

'Yachts are less predictable. These waters are quite dangerous, though, so you don't get too many of those either. But you do get fishing boats – and now they won't see us!'

'A cylinder of invisibility … incredible.' Ben arced a hand in the air. 'And this "Marina" room. Love it.'

Jasmine smiled in agreement. 'It's my favourite place in all of Gemini Force One.'

'I bet they don't have a thing like this at Google.'

'Don't mention that company in front of Truby!'

'I kind of doubt that Jason Truby gives a monkey's about some software rival.'

She shrugged. 'My father says that Truby sees *everyone* as a rival. I guess it's hard to believe it, when we're only seeing his "secret" life, but there's more to Jason Truby than Gemini Force.'

'Why do you think he's doing this? I mean, the entire Gemini Force project … it must have cost, like, a billion dollars.'

'Two billion so far, my dad says – if you count all the aircraft and the submersible.'

'That's a lot of dosh.' Ben was quiet for a moment, reflecting first how Jason Truby's fortune and ambition dwarfed even Casper Carrington's, and then becoming faintly queasy as he remembered how his father's business had ended up.

An awkward silence followed. Ben didn't really want to talk about money. These days it usually made him feel miserable. Before his father had died, money had simply never been an issue. There had always been enough. Now he was just like most people. He'd have to learn to survive on his wits and education.

'I guess you're pretty sad about what's happened to your family.' Jasmine had clearly picked up on what must have seemed like a sudden mood shift.

'It hasn't hit me yet. I'm still away at school; my life hasn't changed much – yet. It'll certainly be a new experience, being broke.'

She looked at him with a curious expression. 'I meant, sad about your father?'

Ben froze with embarrassment. He wasn't used to people actually talking to him about his father's death. In England it could be considered rude. But Jasmine was facing him with a curiously frank, sympathetic expression. 'I thought you were talking about my dad's company going bust,' he said.

'Oh. Did it?'

'Yeah. It's been a bit of a 'mare. We found out after my father died.'

Her next question took him entirely by surprise. 'Are you angry with him?'

'Angry?' He sensed the beginnings of a blush.

'For losing his company. It's OK,' she said, with a shrug. 'Not everyone gets on with their father. I guess you're more of a mother's boy.'

After a solitary, stunned second, Ben said, 'Did you just call me a mummy's boy?'

'I'm sorry, maybe I'm not translating correctly from the German. Or maybe it's, you know, a cultural thing.' She blinked, twice. Apparently, she wasn't joking.

Ben was wondering whether to tell Jasmine that she was actually being rather rude, when his attention was distracted by a movement behind the glass wall adjacent to the lift. It was a floor-to-ceiling window into the medical unit. Inside, Lola Reyes stood waving to Ben and Jasmine, a mischievous grin on her face.

Another woman, at least ten years older, appeared at Lola's side. She had striking, almost stern features, a smooth, pale complexion and black hair tied back in a loose ponytail. Fashionable black-rimmed glasses were perched on her nose, with piercing dark eyes behind.

'Who's that?' he murmured.

'Lola?'

'I know Lola. I meant the other woman.'

'That's Nina Atalas. From Jakarta. She's Chief of Medicine.'

'Huh, all the women on this base are pretty fit.'

Jasmine flashed him a sharp glance. 'Are you saying that's why Truby hired them – for their looks?'

He held up both hands. 'Hey, take it easy! It's a given that they're brilliant, as well.'

'The men here are handsome too, but you don't hear me saying it.'

'You just did.'

She ignored the rebuke. 'I guess you've been brought in as my entertainment.'

Ben recoiled. 'I'm *your* entertainment?'

'Sure you are. British guys are meant to be funny. And already you're kind of making me laugh.'

'Let's swim. I'm wearing my bathing suit underneath my clothes, but you can make do with your shorts.'

Ben smiled. 'Great idea. I was just about to suggest the same thing, but ...'

Blithely she said, 'But you were shy about asking me to undress?'

'Got it in one.'

'I'm Swiss. We're cool about all that stuff.'

'Is that so? You should give a seminar at my school. Guys like me *need* that kind of knowledge.'

Jasmine laughed. 'I think you know it perfectly well. I just assumed you were trying to be an English gentleman.'

'Yes! That! Exactly what I should have said. You're obviously wise beyond your years. By the way, how old is that?'

There was a hint of defiance in her reply. 'Fifteen. And in case you're getting the wrong idea, I have a boyfriend.'

Ben kept his voice deliberately disinterested. 'Oh, yeah? That's cool.'

She asked, 'Do you have a girlfriend?'

'No. I go to an all-boys boarding school. Most of

us don't have girlfriends. Some say they do but, you know, verification can be difficult. I prefer to imagine everyone is as dateless as me.' He finished with a grin that he hoped might conceal how painfully honest he was being.

They'd been swimming for no more than ten minutes when Truby and Caroline appeared at the water's edge. Truby in particular seemed pleased to see the two of them together.

'Good to see you enjoying yourself, Ben. Addison's on the first deck. She's asking if you'd like to take a look around some of the aircraft,' he said.

'Yeah, sure!' Ben grabbed hold of the edge of the pool and pushed himself out in one clean movement.

'I'll keep you company, Jasmine, my dear,' Caroline said. She removed her robe, beneath which was a green-and-black one-piece bathing suit.

Ben picked up his clothes. Deliberately, he turned. The idea was that Truby would follow him out of the room. The nature of his mother's relationship with Truby troubled him. Ben preferred not even to think about it, and Truby gazing admiringly at Caroline in a swimsuit was creeping him out. The sooner they left the Marina room, the better.

Truby escorted Ben to a cabin on the lower, second deck so he could get showered and dressed. 'You're rooming with your mom. We only have one guest cabin. Hope that's OK.'

'No prob,' Ben answered lightly as he went inside.

Truby hadn't moved Caroline in with himself, then. *Excellent news*.

Ben was dressed and sitting in one of the easy chairs watching *Call of Duty* videos on YouTube while he waited for Addison to pick him up for the tour, when his mother returned from the Marina room.

She wrapped an affectionate arm around him. 'Addison's not here yet? That's good; there's something I want to show you. By the way, how did you like Jasmine?'

Ben nodded. 'She's all right, yeah. A bit ...'

His mother smiled. 'Blunt? Direct?'

His eyes widened with relief. 'Yes. *So* direct.'

'I don't want you to be bored while you're staying here.'

'Mum, I could never be bored on GF One.'

'All the same. I'm glad there's someone your age for you to talk to. But I know what you really want is to be useful ...'

'Exactly.'

'... so before you go on your tour of the base with Addi, I've another surprise for you.'

He waited for his mother to throw some clothes on, then followed her upstairs to the upper deck, to the lounge area at the brow of GF One. There, asleep among the chintzy floor cushions that littered the maple-wood floor, lay Rigel. The dog seemed exhausted. He didn't even stir when Ben approached and touched a hand, gently, to Rigel's flopped ear.

In a voice of soft delight Ben said, 'You brought him!'

'His body clock isn't adjusted yet. And he was awake for the entire flight from Austria,' Caroline told him.

'He's jet-lagged? Poor pooch!' Ben's hand caressed Rigel's jaw more firmly until the dog's eyes opened, sleepily at first, then, as a deep intake of breath confirmed Ben's scent, snapping wide open as Rigel staggered to his feet. Then Rigel leaped on Ben, who fell to his knees, hugging the dog and turning his face to avoid the enthusiastic lapping of Rigel's tongue.

'Ugh, stop it, stink-breath!' Ben squeezed the dog around the chest, pressing his cheek against Rigel's neck. Now that he was alert, the dog's writhing, muscular body was shaking with joy. Ben patted Rigel's head firmly enough to lower him onto all fours.

Caroline stood by, content. 'I've decided that Rigel belongs here. I'm not going to be in Austria enough to look after him there. Besides – a dog does great things for morale.'

'Plus, he can be a rescuer!' Ben exclaimed.

She gave a non-committal shrug. 'Maybe, but there's no one to train him. I was thinking more of having him as a pet – a kind of Gemini Force mascot.'

'But he's a working dog! He's happiest when he's helping out. And – hello,' Ben jabbed a finger at his own chest, '*I* can train him.'

'You could,' she said, brightly, 'except that you're going to be away at school. Rigel won't be on the base all the time, anyway. He needs to be walked. Jason and

I are going to take turns taking Rigel back to Jason's place on Cozumel.'

'He can be walked here. Around the base, on the treadmill ... we could find a way.'

Caroline gave a knowing smile. 'You're not staying, Ben.'

'Mum, I'm having a rubbish time at Kenton.'

'Your headmaster says you're making progress.'

'Only because they've stopped me doing anything I actually enjoy.'

'Don't you want to be an officer? You won't get into Sandhurst without decent A-levels at the very least, and, probably, a university degree.'

Ben sat cross-legged on the wooden floor, continuing to nuzzle Rigel. The dog's tail hadn't stopped wagging since he'd seen Ben.

'Fair point. But I hate studying,' he told his mum. 'You should be glad I'm not like half the boys I know who just want to mess around and chase girls. They don't have any plans for their future – apart from living off their parents, one way or another. I just want to be doing something useful. To start my career. Now!'

There was a brief pause as Caroline absorbed this. 'I hear what you're saying, Ben. But I can't help feeling that if your father were alive, you wouldn't have argued.'

That much was true and Ben knew it. He kept silent for a moment, remembering how little interest his father had ever shown in his son's opinions. Casper always, *always* knew best. Everyone else was ill-informed or simply stupid. He'd always claimed that his worldview had built Carrington International into one of the world's biggest hotel brands.

But it had all been a sham. Ben didn't really understand how it was that Casper and his chief financial officer had deceived the rest of the board of Carrington International. Yet it was clear enough that, at some crucially important stage, Casper had lied to people who'd trusted him.

It made Ben doubt everything his father had ever said. Maybe it had all been lies. What should he care, then, about his father's wishes for his education?

To Caroline he only said, in a tired voice, 'Whatever.'

An ear-splitting klaxon sounded then, three times. It jerked Ben and his mother to attention. Around them, members of Gemini Force began to race towards the upper deck. The initial burst of noise was replaced by a recording of Jason's voice saying calmly, 'Gemini Force, to the command centre.'

Caroline stood and looked expectantly at Ben. 'Stand by for action!'

⚊ SCORPIO ⚊

The second they arrived at the command centre, Truby turned to Caroline. 'You ready for a ride-along? Julia's going to do some recon with *Scorpio*, take Paul in the firefighter suit. We may decide to carry out a bigger intervention.'

Ben said, 'You mean a rescue?'

'Maybe. Sometimes it's not about rescuing people in present danger, but more about making sure that the threat doesn't escalate.'

Ben looked closely at each element of the rescuers' uniform. The helmet in particular attracted his attention. There was a small, stud-like feature on the front.

Julia noticed him looking. 'It's a camera,' she told him. 'All our rescues are relayed back via video link. The crew can see everything that's going on and advise.'

'It's all about having eyes on the situation,' Truby said. 'The more the better.' He stepped back a little then, making space for Addison and Caroline as they lined up next to Julia beside one of the exit gates around the edge of the main deck.

Ben watched for a second, then followed. The airlock was open by the time he reached the gate. Julia ushered

Addison and Caroline through. She put up a hand to stop Ben.

'Oh, come on,' he said, a touch irritated. 'I can watch!'

Julia shot a glance at Truby. The response must have been good, because she lowered her arm. Ben pushed past, through the airlock.

He found himself in a generous aircraft hangar pod. It was dominated by a helicopter as long as a small passenger aircraft. The body shape was somewhere between a helicopter and an aeroplane. It had two chunky rotor blades at either end of what might have been wings, stubby protrusions from the main body of the craft. The paintwork was a dark, matte blue-grey. No distinctive markings. If he'd had to guess, Ben would have said that the helicopter looked military.

As he rounded the vehicle, Ben saw inside. Paul was wearing some kind of protective metal suit, part reinforced and robotic, part protective armour. The arms and legs were twice the size of Paul's legs. There seemed to be jetpacks attached to the ankles and to the suit's back. With just one arm encased in metal, Paul appeared to be using his free arm to attach a spool of fire hose to a generous tool belt on the suit's hip.

'What are you, Iron Man?' Ben asked as he climbed into the helicopter. Paul didn't reply. He was too focused.

Julia had already led Caroline to the cockpit, leaving Addison and Ben with Paul in the main part of the craft. As in a military transport chopper, there were rows of seats along each side of the cabin. Ben and Addison strapped themselves in.

Ben sat, fascinated, as Paul completed his preparations. The final step seemed to be anchoring himself to a magnetic coupling on the wall. When Paul hit a switch on the right forearm of the suit, he clunked noisily against the side of the helicopter, pinned in place.

The doors to the aircraft began to close. The entire hangar began to rise. After a few seconds Ben heard water rushing as they broke the surface of the ocean. Sunlight shot through the hangar pod as the ceiling rolled aside.

Julia started up the rotors. Within a minute the whole helicopter was vibrating gently, the thrum of the blades so loud now that you couldn't hear the intercom. Ben glanced to his left. Small wireless headsets hung on metal pegs next to every seat. The speakers were in-ear, the microphone a soft foam-coated blob the size of a bee.

Ben put his headset on. He flipped a switch near the right speaker. Instantly, all background noise reduced to a faint hum. He heard Julia talking to Truby in the command centre. They were discussing the mission.

An oil refinery in the Dominican Republic had reported an explosion of unknown cause. There was some indication that the flames were spreading beyond the capability of the local fire crew. Julia might use *Scorpio*'s water cannons to help out. Paul could use the suit to access any tricky locations. There were no reports of casualties so far, but if the flames reached the oil storage tank then the situation would instantly change. The entire neighbourhood would have to be evacuated.

They were in the air. Through the tinted windows of *Scorpio*, Ben saw the deep turquoise blue of the Caribbean Sea. They flew low enough to see white caps on the waves.

He gazed longingly at Paul's biomechanical firefighting suit.

Maybe one day.

A second voice, not Truby's, came over the radio. 'The explosion took out the blowdown drum. No information on what caused it. The flames are so close to the isomerisation unit that the fire engines can't get close. It's already so hot that the temperature inside the ISOM unit is getting dangerously high. They've shut off the furnace and closed down the flow of raffinate into the ISOM. But a way has to be found to lower the temperature, else it'll overheat, overflow and the blowdown fire will get a fresh hit of fuel. Over.'

'Who's that?' Ben whispered to Paul, who replied, 'James Winch. I don't think you've met him yet. He's our geological engineer.'

'What he's saying about the refinery – it sounds bad,' Ben said. 'I *think* I get the basic idea. We did petroleum cracking in chemistry. Raffinate is the derivate from crude oil, right? And it's overheating inside the tank or whatever? What's the blowdown drum?'

Paul didn't answer, lost in his own concentration, adjusting something on each thick arm of the suit. A wall-mounted HDTV screen came to life. The display showed an animated schematic of the oil refinery. Arrows appeared over the 'ISOM' and 'blowdown'. To Ben, these looked like drum-shaped towers. The blowdown was narrower and topped with a vertical spout. In the animation this was shown as a fireball. His interest was immediately ignited in a way that it had never been when he'd had to pore over schematic diagrams in chemistry GCSE.

This time Truby spoke, talking them through the visuals. 'The ISOM is this wider tower. It's about fifty metres high and it fills from the base with heated hydrocarbons – the "raffinate", Ben, as you correctly pointed out.'

Ben breathed a quick sigh of relief that he'd managed to give a fair impression of the knowledge he'd gleaned in chemistry lessons. It was tough to be around all these super-clever Gemini Force types. He'd have to be at the top of his game at all times.

James Winch's voice took over again. 'The heated hydrocarbons are cracked down into smaller molecules. The higher you go, the more volatile they get. Heat and volatility is a super-bad combination. The fires are close enough to make that whole area dangerously hot.'

'Here's the plan,' Truby said. 'The onsite crew are trying to put out the fire. Right now, they've got one water cannon on the ISOM. They badly need to switch that cannon over to the main fire. *Capricorn*, use the suit to go in, fly close enough to the tower and cool it at the base where the flow goes in. That's where it's hottest. *Scorpio*, use the water cannon to help out where needed. Over.'

Ben heard Julia reply, 'Roger that, *Gemini*. *Scorpio* prepped for intervention. Over and out.'

It seemed he was about to discover what Gemini Force was all about.

⏤ ANPECO ⏤

The screen began to show possible approaches to the refinery. Paul was still working on the arms of his suit.

Ben asked, 'You got fire extinguishers in there?'

'The arms are basically cylinders of liquid nitrogen,' Paul explained. 'There are nozzles in the wrists so I can flip up my hands to release jets of super-freezing vapour. It won't put out a fire once it's got going but, as an instant coolant for a localised spot, it's as good as it gets.'

'What's the localised bit that you need to cool down?'

'At the base of the tower there are sensors that send information to the control room. They got a bit fried, so they're sending the wrong information right now. I'm going to take a shot at cooling the sensors enough to get them functional.'

Addison looked on with detached interest. She asked Paul a couple of technical questions about the suit, about his experience with fires. When he replied, she made little response but seemed to just file the information away.

Ben didn't even try to strike up conversation with her. All that came to mind were jokey asides that, when he imagined saying them in front of a veteran of the war in Afghanistan, sounded pretty lame. Besides which, he was far too distracted by trying to imagine what Paul must be thinking and feeling right now. What if the suit failed? Compared to the sleek Iron Man suit from the comic books, it looked clunky. He had to remind himself that this was a real, functioning piece of equipment. Presumably it had been tested and found to perform. Yet Ben was finding it hard to believe it would actually fly.

He tried to remember if he'd been nervous or anxious when he fell from the edge of the Sky-High. He couldn't. It made him wonder if he'd blanked something about the experience. Even now, months later, Ben found it hard to confront the memory directly. Every time he approached it he could feel a thread of nausea pulling through him.

The suit *had* to fly. In equal measures, Ben dreaded and felt thrilled by the prospect of watching Paul leap out of *Scorpio*.

The image on-screen had switched to a flight map. It showed satellite views of their progress in a line through the Caribbean. They were carving a path between Cuba's southern coast and the island of Jamaica.

A different voice crackled over the radio: '*Scorpio*, you are cleared to enter Haitian airspace. Proceed direct to the ANPECO refinery at Bajos de Haina, located on the coast five klicks west of Santo Domingo.'

The time passed incredibly fast. Between the constant flow of information to the screen and over the airwaves,

Paul had few breaks for conversation. As *Scorpio* began to descend, he did find time to crack a grin.

'Wish me luck. I've spent about twenty-five training hours in this suit, but I've never done anything quite like this.'

Julia's voice said, 'Opening doors now.'

'Good luck!' Ben told Paul.

The brilliant green of the Dominican countryside burst into view below them. As the helicopter descended even further, Ben could see the pillar of black smoke that rose from a widespread concreted area near the sea. It was surrounded by a more dispersed cloud of whiter smoke. They went closer, changed trajectory, headed for the coast. Now and then, within the smoke cloud, Ben caught glimpses of an orange interior of flames.

'Respirators,' said Julia. Panels opened in the wall against which Ben and Addison were sitting. 'Take the mask to your right. Put it on. We're flying close enough that you're gonna need them.'

Ben stared at the billows of dense, creamy smoke. Inside, it had to be getting hellish. Steam and smoke and flames, all mixed together. He watched Addison pull the breathing mask into place over her face, then followed her lead.

Across from him, Paul was putting on a light helmet, respirator and finally a flame-resistant hood with a wraparound visor that was coated in a metallic, copper-coloured material. Presumably the helmet would move freely inside the looser fire hood.

Paul spoke over the intercom. '*Capricorn* ready. Passengers secured with breathing equipment. We're good to go.'

'Distance to the ANPECO refinery is two nautical miles,' Julia responded. 'Visibility within the smoke cloud is poor. Suggest you engage infrared vision – turned right down, 'cause that fireball in the middle might blow the sensors out.'

'Roger that. I'll release the magnetic hold on your signal ... Good to go.'

'I'm as close as I want to get without engaging the water cannon. Your suit should have enough flight time to get in quick and cool down that ISOM. Set the countdown timer, though. Leave yourself enough time to get back.'

'Certainly will do that, *Scorpio*. I don't fancy ending up on the barbie.'

'*Capricorn*, you're clear to fly.'

Ben, Addison and Paul stared through the now-open door at the rolling smoke less than fifty metres away. The fire within and the hiss of steam mingled with the pulsing cannons of water below in one loud sustained roar.

'Oh, well,' Ben heard Paul say, 'better get going.'

The magnetic hold which had previously gripped the suit somewhere around the thighs, suddenly released Paul. He staggered for a second, then moved clunkily, like someone walking in ski boots, to the edge of the open helicopter. The jetpack on his back ignited with a popping sound. The flame plume was squat and tightly contained, but Ben felt an instant pulse of heat, even metres away.

Paul stepped off the edge and dropped out of sight but, two seconds later, Ben could see the suit flying him on a diagonal rise, arrows of flame spurting from his ankles and the jetpack on his back. Another second and he was gone – enveloped within the mixture of steam and black smoke.

Scorpio followed him into the cloud.

'Watch the screen,' Ben heard Julia say. 'You can see the feed from *Capricorn*'s helmet cam.'

The screen was barely visible through the smoke that had penetrated the cabin but Ben saw that the field of vision being filmed by *Capricorn*'s camera was erratic. Huge flares of light dominated every couple of seconds. Gradually Ben became aware that they were seeing the ISOM drum, over which Paul was hovering. Dark shadows flowed from the hands in front of the camera – the hands of the firefighting suit. The shadows shot across the screen. They enveloped the tower, gobbling up the brightness.

Abruptly, the tower appeared to topple to one side. It took Ben a few seconds to register that Paul must have fallen and now lay on his side, his helmet cam pointed straight at the ISOM drum. Red LED lights shone in front of the camera. A number. It hung in the air: an omen.

0:35

Ben said, 'Isn't that the suit's power indicator? It looks like Paul's only got thirty-five seconds of flight time left!'

➤ OXYGEN ➤

'Nice going, *Capricorn*,' Truby said. 'We're getting reports from ANPECO that the tower's no longer in danger of a second explosion. Now you'd better get out of there so that *Scorpio* can join the other firefighters dousing the flames.'

'Roger that, *Gemini*,' Julia said.

There was a momentary silence on the radio waves. Then Julia urged, '*Capricorn*, please respond.'

Nothing.

Addison said, 'Maybe he's overheated?'

'Suit internal temperature is within viable limits,' responded Julia, via the intercom.

'Something's wrong,' Ben said. 'We need to get him out of there.'

Addison began to unbuckle her restraints. 'Kid's right. Julia, you gotta land.'

'No landing,' Julia said. 'I need a *Scorpio*-sized hole, at least, or those flames are going to frazzle our systems and we'll be trapped on the ground.'

Addison stood. 'Then put me down with a rope. There's enough of a gap for that. He's got thirty-five seconds' flight time on his jetpack. I'll use it to bring us both up.'

'Get an isotherm jacket on under your uniform, first,' came back Julia's voice, 'or the heat will fry you after a few minutes.'

Ben blurted, 'There's no time for that! She's got to get in and out as fast as she can.'

Assuming Paul is still alive to rescue, he thought. Something had made the man tumble. Now – to judge by the feed on the screen – he wasn't moving. The LED timer on his wrist remained in view, confirming just over half a minute of juice left in the tanks.

Ben heard Caroline's voice. 'Can you water the wider area? That might reduce the temperature for long enough.'

'Good idea,' Ben agreed. 'It might buy them a few minutes of extra time before the heat gets unbearable.'

Ben undid his restraints; there had to be something he could do. 'Let me help.'

Caroline shouted across the intercom, 'Benedict Carrington, you just stay where you are. It's dangerous!'

'Your mom's got a point,' said Addison.

Scorpio dipped a couple of metres. 'This is as low as we're going,' Julia announced. 'I'm directing the water cannon in a circle around Paul. I can't risk soaking him because it'll damage the jetpack. Addison, I'm opening a panel in the ceiling, just beside the door. You'll find an anchored rope with leg straps inside. Put it on. I'll get in close enough to put you on the ground, but the flames are too close for me to stay at that height for long.'

'Don't worry 'bout that,' Addison said. 'Just get me on

the ground, but stay close. I'll fly him back but thirty-five seconds' flight time doesn't leave a lot of leeway.'

He could hear the faint disbelief in Julia's delayed response. 'You really think you can fly the suit, when you're not even wearing it?'

Addison shrugged. 'Just tell me how to turn on the jets. I've had enough parachuting and freefall experience to adjust for whatever movements the jets cause. It might take me a couple of tries to get it just right.'

'I've seen her fly,' Truby confirmed, over the radio. 'If anyone can do it, Addi can.'

'Anyhow,' Addison said, 'I'm going to have to try. There's no time to get Paul out of the suit. Neither of us will last long enough in that heat.'

Julia said, 'OK. The suit has an emergency override via a control pad on the inside left arm. You can't miss it. Up, down, left, right. You steer by leaning.' A pause. 'I'm sorry, Addi. It's the kind of thing you have to train for to do really well.'

Ben heard Addison's breathing reverberate inside her respirator. Behind his own mask, he stared at her with wide eyes.

'You should douse yourself first,' he said. 'It's pretty toasty down there.'

'That's a great idea,' returned Julia. 'There's a panel marked with a HAZMAT symbol, just opposite your seats. You'll find a fire hose inside. Use it to soak yourself. But hold on to something, in case the water pressure blows you out of the chopper. Ben – strap into your seat!'

Addison opened the panel and tugged on a metal cylinder that then pulled out a short length of hose. She glanced once at Ben, then handed him the end of the hose. Then she touched a button on the side of her helmet. A red LED light turned on – her helmet camera.

'Get ready to hit it, kid.'

Ben watched Addison find the ceiling panel and push the release catch. In the next minute she was climbing into the rope harness. He tried to think through everything she'd have to do. This was his first training opportunity. Every little thing he observed might come in useful, some day.

She had to get herself soaked, reach the ground, find Paul, get him on his feet and activate the jetpack – all this in the few minutes Addison would have before the water *Scorpio* doused the area with had turned to steam and blown away and the temperature started to rise again.

Flying back to the chopper would be the hardest part. Ben wondered if anyone in Gemini Force would even dare attempt flying the suit while it was worn by someone else. Ben remembered how Addison had sliced through the air towards the pinnacle of the Sky-High Hotel. He'd never seen anyone with better aerial control.

Addison gripped a handle next to the HAZMAT panel. She turned to him. 'OK – now.'

Ben activated the fire hose. A powerful stream leaped

across *Scorpio's* cabin, solid as a sword. In two seconds, Addison was drenched.

'OK, enough! Julia, drop the rope. Make it fast!' Addison instructed.

Holding on to the rope from which she was now suspended, Addison stepped out of the helicopter.

Over the radio in *Scorpio's* cockpit, a harried, Spanish male voice spoke in heavily accented English, 'Civilian helicopter, this is ANPECO Control. Thank you for your assistance. Can you direct water to the ISOM tower? Temperature readings are increasing again. Over.'

'ANPECO Control, copy that. We need to retrieve our man first. Will comply in two minutes,' Julia responded.

'Civilian helicopter, we don't *have* two minutes!' erupted the voice. 'The tower could go critical at any second! We've got to cool it down!'

Ben watched the screen as it flickered into action, displaying the feed from Addi's helmet camera. She was being lowered through clouds of steaming air.

'*Capricorn,* please respond. Over,' Julia tried again.

Nothing.

Julia's frustration was evident even over the airwaves. 'Addi, are you on the ground yet?'

It was hard to make anything out on the screen. The air was a maelstrom of smoke. Finally, Ben heard Addison's voice.

'*Scorpio*, you're clear to move. Can you spray water

over on the other side of the ISOM? We gotta try to keep the jetpack dry.'

'Roger. Go find *Capricorn* for us, Addi.'

The air above Addison stirred into a whirlwind as *Scorpio* swooped upwards and around to the other side of the towering ISOM, which was almost invisible through the pallor of smoke.

Ben couldn't help but imagine himself transported down there. The screen showed a close, imposing darkness and there was a cascade of sounds almost as terrifying as the heat. Black, oily smoke and the cores of each fire flared in every direction.

'*Scorpio*, can you give me a position for *Capricorn*? I can't see a damn thing down here,' Addison said.

'According to the infrared, he's no more than five metres away from you at about two o'clock, but I'm getting a lot of signal bounce from the fires so that could be wrong.'

Ben watched as Addison moved forwards. Ten steps away and on the ground, the hazy shape of Paul's unresponsive form appeared through the smoke.

— FLYGIRL —

Addison's helmet camera tipped down. Ben could see that she now stood behind Paul's head. She bent, lifted his fire hood. Paul's eyes were closed. He looked to be unconscious.

A tremendous hissing sound exploded from somewhere close.

'What the heck is that?' Ben asked.

Julia hesitated, then said, 'It's probably the water we've just released. It's pretty much turning to steam. She's going to have to get out of there fast, or she'll poach.'

Addison, hurry. Ben didn't dare to say it aloud. She was already under insane pressure. But for some reason she was hesitating. Ben's eyes were glued to the screen. What was taking her so long?

In stunned silence Ben watched Addison pull off her own respirator and then Paul's.

'What are you doing?'

There was no reply. *Of course,* thought Ben. *Her radio microphone is probably embedded in the face mask.*

Ben watched as Paul's face mask approached the helmet camera. Addison was swapping masks with Paul.

Was Paul's respirator faulty? Ben peered at the tiny

part of the screen that displayed Paul's face. Was he already dead?

Then the mask was off Addison again. She was turning it over in her hands. Ben guessed that she was trying to find an obvious fault. She put it back on.

Probably no other choice.

'She can't talk,' Ben said, suddenly understanding. 'There's something wrong with the mask. She's got to save her oxygen for breathing. Addi, if you can hear us and you're OK, give us a thumbs-up in front of the camera!'

Tensely he waited until, after a few seconds, Addison's gloved right thumb flashed onto the screen.

Ben thudded back into his seat. He let out a breath with a puff, surprised at how caught up he was getting in Addison's experience. The microphone was picking up the sounds of her breathing. Air was coming unsteadily now. Ben tried not to think about how light-headed she must already be feeling.

Now she was crouching over Paul's prone body. Ben guessed that there wasn't time to check if he was still alive, nor to try CPR. She simply couldn't risk exposing him to the air. Ben could see that it was filling up with hot steam that was billowing around from the other side of the ISOM unit.

They were in a sauna.

When she'd managed to get Paul to his feet, supporting his weight almost entirely, Ben watched as Addison wrapped one leg around Paul's, above the ankle jet. She used her right hand to reach the inside of his left arm. Via the helmet camera, Ben could see the control panel for the jetpack, just as Julia had described. He watched Addison press the 'up' arrow.

The suit shot about ten metres into the air. It appeared to be totally out of control.

'The jetpack control responds to pressure!' screamed Julia over the radio.

Ben could see nothing but opaque grey all around Addison and Paul. He waited, perfectly still, until he saw them burst into the sunlight above the cloud of smoke.

Addison and Paul were about one hundred metres away from *Scorpio*. But they appeared to be flying on a course set to miss by several metres. Ben saw Addison lean hard to her right. To his horror, instead of correcting the trajectory, they began to fall.

Underneath the suit, the jets fired. Ben undid his seatbelt and grabbed hold of a hand rail. He pulled himself to the open door of the helicopter.

'Addison!' he called.

The Addison–Paul unit was zooming in fast. sixty metres, fifty, forty, twenty.

'Cut your speed!' yelled Julia.

Ben held tight and leaned out as far as he dared to watch their approach.

It was too late. They were going to overshoot.

'Julia, you need to correct for them,' Ben shouted. 'Move right by five metres!' He felt the air around him shift as *Scorpio* pitched sideways.

Addison and Paul were above the helicopter now, just metres away. They began the arc of descent.

Ben watched from the door. His hair stood on end in the wind current. They were still going to miss the opening. Helpless, he watched them fall.

But then Addison's arm shot out. She grabbed the tubular landing skid on the base of the helicopter. Somehow she managed to throw her second arm around Paul's body, trapping him between her and the skid. Her face turned upwards until she was staring Ben directly in the eye. She couldn't talk but Ben could sense her desperation.

She wouldn't be able to hold on for long. He had to help.

It was almost exactly like the scenario on the Sky-High – Addison dangling precariously far above the ground, clinging to an unconscious pilot. Only, this time, it was up to Ben to complete the rescue, on a moving helicopter. He glanced around. The rope Addison had used to lower herself to the ground trailed near the opening. Ben made a quick one-handed bowline knot to secure his left wrist, then lowered himself onto the landing skid. He could feel his cheeks furrowing in the wind from the rotor blades. The ground below was entirely invisible beneath thick oily smoke and blasts of white steam.

If he wasn't strong enough to hold her and Addison's weight dragged him down, all three of them would die.

Ben's fingers tightened around his safety rope as he edged out onto the landing skid.

The fingers of Addison's left hand gave way. Her hand slipped off the skid.

Ben threw himself forward, wrapping his legs around the landing skid as though it were a piece of gym equipment. Worst-case scenario, he'd have to hang by his knees.

Now he was directly above Addison.

'I'm going to take your hand,' he shouted. 'Addi, trust me!'

Solid as a rock, he grabbed hold of her right hand just as Addi lost her grip. He began to tug hard, screaming with the effort of pulling two people up. The sensation was like having his arm slowly torn out of its socket but he kept pulling until Addison could get hold of the landing skid.

'Wrap your legs around the skids!' he urged. 'Hold on!'

Now that he was this far out of the helicopter and had three of his limbs wrapped around the tubular skids, Ben's muscles seemed to have gone into spasm. No part of him wanted to move until he was back on the ground.

The three of them clung on for what seemed like ages, eyes narrowed to tiny slits to protect them from the acrid smoke as the helicopter sank lower. Julia flew *Scorpio* down to a car park. There were fire engines and ambulances everywhere. As they neared the ground, Ben jumped off the landing skid. *Scorpio* hovered, just one metre off the ground.

With outstretched arms, Ben pulled Paul to safety.

Addison rolled off the skid, falling heavily to the ground. Ben watched as, with slow, clumsy movements, she pulled off her mask. She took heavy breaths, gasping with obvious relief.

Ben removed Paul's face mask and gazed intently at his face. He put his fingers to the pilot's neck, locating the jugular, then turned to Addison, stunned, relieved.

'Paul's breathing!'

She peered up at him wearily. A steady grin appeared on her face. 'Kid, the only reason either of us is breathing is *you*.'

～ AQUARIUS ～

It didn't take Addison long to make her feelings known. As soon as they landed back on Gemini Force One, she went directly over to Truby, who was on the main deck, waiting to greet them.

'What kind of garbage equipment are you sending your people out with?' she demanded.

'Addison,' Truby said calmly. 'It's not possible to test every new system in every single unforeseen circumstance. These are state-of-the-art respirators, and they perform well – as evidenced by your mask and Ben's. The problem seems to be the interface with the jetpack suit – the mixture of smoke and steam. It caused Paul's mask to malfunction. We don't know how exactly, but we will find out. Having said all that, I respect your attitude.'

'Huh. Sounds like you use that line a *lot*.'

'I don't get too many employees bawling me out, actually,' Truby replied.

'Well, Mr Truby, I'm not sure I'm sticking around any longer.'

'I wish you would.'

'I'd rather stay alive.'

'For someone who takes the kind of risks that you take, Addison, that's an even bet at best.'

'If I'm going to bet, I prefer not to play with loaded dice.'

'All right, point taken. So what should I do?'

For the first time, Ben noticed Addison's confidence falter. Truby's question seemed to knock some air out of her.

'Hey, that's not my problem,' she said at last.

'What if it was?'

'How could it be?'

'Addison, stop playing games. I know enough about you to know that the Air Force was all you ever wanted to do. For reasons that I still don't understand, you gave all that up. I only know that Gemini Force has to be staffed with the best. And you, Addison, you've seen more battle and flown more hours than anyone here. This is the right place for you and I respect your opinion. So, you tell me – not what you think I want to hear, but the truth. What do we need to do?'

She paused for a moment. 'You gotta stop expecting people to do all their own safety testing. Hire a couple more staff. People who'll inspect all the stuff, every last thing that goes into each rescue vehicle – right down to the needle and thread in the first-aid kit.'

Truby nodded. 'You got it. Anything we need to keep everyone safe. The key thing to remember is that Paul accomplished his mission – he cooled the base of the blowdown drum. And there wasn't another explosion.

We helped contain the fire. You got Paul out and Ben performed admirably.'

That was the last thing Ben heard of their rather robust discussion – and then only in the background – because he'd already started discreetly to retreat. Still, it was good to know that Truby had noticed his contribution.

Ben was halfway to the guest cabin when Addison caught up with him.

'Hey, kid. You all recovered?' she asked.

'Me? I'm fine. You're the one who's been threatening to leave,' he told her.

She smiled. 'Every so often you gotta push the boss to talk you into staying.'

Ben said, 'What if they don't?'

She pulled a face. 'Jeez, don't I *hate* when that happens? Anyhow, listen; I never did get to give you that tour of the base. But Truby says I can show you something *very* cool.'

Addison didn't stick around to talk, but immediately turned to lead Ben through the base. They headed directly for one of four exit gates that he knew led to aircraft hangar pods. It wasn't the one they'd used last time to access *Scorpio*.

Ben was about to see his second Gemini Force vehicle.

This time, Addison didn't wait for any kind of countdown to the exit gates opening. Instead she touched a panel in the wall and entered a code. He heard a sound like the approach of a lift.

'What's this one – GF Three? Four?'

He looked sheepish as Addison tapped the mission patch on her jacket, which she wore unzipped. It clearly showed the number four.

'Truby calls the airplane *Aquarius*. You'll soon see why.'

The hangar pod was about half the size of the one that housed *Scorpio*. In the middle was a small craft, no more than a six-seater. It was sleek of form, with broad, stubby wings and a propeller attached to the front of the tail. A body of dazzling chrome reflected the relatively drab surroundings of the hangar. It seemed shiny, but nothing special. Ben had hoped for something a bit more sci-fi.

'*This* is Truby's most expensive aeroplane?' he asked doubtfully.

Addison smirked. 'Wait up.' She headed for the cockpit and leaned in until only her legs remained outside.

Before Ben's eyes, the surface of the aircraft began to shimmer. The light seemed to shift around it. And then he was staring into space – and at a neatly bisected Addison suspended in mid-air.

Ben took a single step forward. 'It's got an invisibility shield?'

Addison emerged as if from another dimension. A knowing grin was spread across her features. 'Better. The invisibility thing they got to cloak the base is cylinder-shaped. It actually bends light, but you got no cover from overhead. And it only lasts for a few minutes. Now this is something totally different – *camouflage*. Come closer. Touch it.'

Ben approached, until he was standing next to where Addison's arm seemed to have disappeared into a black hole in mid-air. Now that he was right next to it, he saw a clear shimmer. After a few seconds, his eyes adjusted. Hanging in the air was textured light, in the shape of a small plane.

'It looks transparent …' he breathed. His voice felt like an echo.

'*Aquarius*,' Addison said happily. 'The water carrier.'

'How does it work?'

'Whole plane is covered with LED plaques. Tiny hi-res screens. And cameras. So many eyes, it's like some crazy insect. Each camera picks up an image of what's directly behind the airplane at the exact position of each plaque. Then the on-board computer creates a smooth image over the whole craft. It works like the human eye – where there's no exact information, maybe in an overlap, the imaging software makes something up.'

Tentatively, Ben reached out to touch the light-rippled surface. His fingers felt a smooth, matte metal, alternating with frequent, yet invisible, ridges. 'Perfect camouflage! This is amazing. I knew they'd been working on this tech for tanks. It stops them getting picked up by night-vision goggles. I had no idea that the tech was this far advanced!'

Addison checked her watch. 'Time to go. We should both get some rest. That was a heavy day.'

Ben watched the camouflage dissipate at the touch of Addison's fingers on the control panel inside *Aquarius*. The gleaming aeroplane appeared to materialise out of thin air.

He'd rather have stayed to see more. But Addison was right – he was exhausted. Not to mention starving. He was already mentally assembling a sandwich.

The entire crew was up at seven the next morning for some pre-breakfast *krav maga* training. Ben had watched a demonstration of the Israeli combat technique at school, when a former pupil who'd gone on to serve in the Israeli army had visited to recruit students to a kibbutz programme. Ben had tried a few different hand-to-hand fighting techniques, but hadn't taken anything up. His father had used this as evidence that Ben wasn't serious about being a soldier.

'The army will train me,' Ben used to insist. 'And my reasons for wanting to join up have nothing to do with fighting.' Then, because Casper so often liked to use the same source, Ben would quote Sun Tzu's *The Art of War*. '*The supreme art of war is to subdue the enemy without fighting.*'

The lift returned them to the lower deck. Tim and Paul were just leaving their cabin as Addison caught up with them. Both were wearing grey T-shirts and cargo pants.

'I'm going to have to kick your butt,' Tim told Paul, deadpan.

'You can try it,' Paul replied, solemnly. 'But I excel in the art of running away.'

Ben asked, 'Addi – did your training include any hand-to-hand combat?'

'Not me – just survival and evasion. Plus I can shoot an M16.'

Tim gave a cheerful grin. 'So I'm gonna kick *all* your butts.'

They arrived in the gym. Truby was there as well as Ben's mother. Both were barefoot and dressed in the Gemini Force One uniform, minus jacket.

Facing them was someone that Ben hadn't seen before: a man in his late thirties, well muscled and, at six feet tall, the same height as Ben. The man's hair was fair, and he had icy-blue eyes with eyebrows heavily pronounced, giving an impression of intense focus. He hadn't shaved for at least three days. An amused grin played around his lips as he surveyed the latest arrivals.

'You must be Ben,' he said, offering a hand. 'Great work down there at the refinery, by the way! I'm James Winch. I moonlight as the team's combat trainer. So you're the bloke who wants to join the army?'

'That's right.'

'I was in the army for about six years.' James shook his head. 'It can get pretty grim, war.'

Ben frowned. This sounded like a speech for his mother's benefit.

James continued. 'Is it the armed forces in general? Or do you specifically want to be a "ground-pounder"?'

Truby and his mother seemed keen to hear the answer. James moved closer, an obvious incursion into Ben's personal space. Ben didn't give way.

'I'd prefer to be on the ground, if that's what you mean. I think you can do more to protect people that way.'

James gave him a playful shove. 'Oh, yeah? Why not join the police?'

Ben rocked slightly from the attack. He glanced at his mother once again, but her eyes conveyed nothing but amusement. Was James trying to prove a point? He bent his knees slightly, transferred his weight to the balls of his feet. This time, when James's hands came in for a heavier push, Ben shifted right, dodging the attack with just millimetres to spare.

Tim and Paul laughed. James just nodded approvingly.

'Good. You already know the first rule. If someone wants to get into a fight with you, get out of the way.'

'What if they're hurting someone I'm trying to protect?' Ben asked.

'Well, Ben, if you absolutely insist on being a knight in shining armour, you'd better learn how to fight.'

ISIDORE

Ben was the first to spot the distress signal around noon. Some of the crew were still showering after the *krav maga* session. The whole thing had turned into a bit of a showcase for James as well as Truby, whose sparring with Caroline had bordered on flirting. It wasn't something that Ben had found easy to witness.

Ben himself hadn't even had a chance to break a sweat, so he certainly wasn't going to waste his precious last few hours on the base taking a shower. Tim was showing him how the global information feeds could be monitored in the command centre.

Tim and Ben were the only people there. An array of screens gazed down on a semi-circular arrangement of seats. Two screens were devoted simply to collating a series of newsfeeds from a range of sources: the emergency frequencies that all rescue services monitored, a special line that Truby had established for what Tim could only call 'high-level access', as well as Twitter and Facebook.

Tim was debating the merits of different social networks for finding people who might be in danger, when Ben noticed something flash up at the bottom of the Twitter feed.

'What about this?' he said, pointing at the screen. '*Caught an SOS via the Caribbean Maritime Mobile Net. Sounded like a sailor in trouble. I'm in Jamaica. Anyone else hear it?*' He turned to Tim. 'Maritime Mobile Net. What's that?'

Tim replied curtly, 'Sounds like one of the ham radio operators. They monitor shortwave radio and communicate. They're hobbyists but they take it pretty seriously. It's often one of them that spots someone in danger.'

'The Caribbean ... So the signal came from a boat in our neighbourhood, right?'

Tim moved across the array of screens and stopped in front of the one in the bottom right. He pointed at the screen, which showed satellite maps. He went swiftly to the control desk, tapped a keyboard and changed the satellite view. Now they were looking at a swirl of white cloud above the ocean. He took a sharp breath.

'Hello ... where did you come from? You look like a right wee troublemaker.'

'Is it a storm?' Ben asked.

'It is.' Tim was fully alert now. Within the next two minutes he'd scanned three more screens and made a quick call via a Bluetooth headset. 'We've got a weather warning in the Caribbean. Looks like they may be about to upgrade it to a tropical cyclone. The name will be ... Isidore. Sounds innocent enough, but don't be fooled.'

'What about the distress call?'

'The satellite images are already suggesting winds of around a hundred and eighty kilometres per hour.

The area affected is pretty small,' Tim said. He added, ominously, 'For now, that is. Can be a nasty bit of water, the Caribbean.'

'Gemini Force should do something – don't you think?'

'We should certainly gear up, aye,' Tim said. He pressed a red button on the control panel. The lighting on the entire deck flicked from moody and subdued to glaring bright. A recording of Jason's voice began to play over a loudspeaker system. His voice sounded calmer than his words.

'Gemini Force, to the command centre.'

Three minutes later, Tim, Paul, Toru, Addison and Julia took seats in the semi-circle of fixed, rotating easy chairs that faced the bank of computer screens and the control panel.

Michael Dietz and James Winch arrived at roughly the same time. They immediately began to navigate the screens and airwaves. Ben guessed that they were verifying what Tim had found, and following up. A couple of minutes later, Jason entered with Caroline. He gave Ben a friendly grin.

'Take a seat, Ben. Why don't you watch how we do this?'

Wordlessly, Ben obeyed. Caroline took the seat next to his. She smiled and squeezed his arm. 'Turn on your computer. Dietz and James will relay any key data to it.'

Ben touched the small, tablet-sized screen that was embedded in the left arm of his chair. Instantly, it came to life. The display was initially incomprehensible – just a steady stream of numbers. He looked up, hopefully. No one seemed to be about to explain anything. Even Caroline seemed to understand exactly what the data meant. After ten minutes of listening in on the team's conversations, Ben began to see that the numbers were wind speeds, wave heights, coordinates.

Dietz spoke up. 'I've found another reference to the original SOS. Another tweeter. This one is in Caracas, Venezuela. Another radio ham. He managed to hear some of the coordinates.'

Truby asked, 'Is it enough to go on?'

'It's enough to make a good guess. If there's a sailing boat in trouble out there, I wouldn't give much for their chances in the next two hours. That storm's going nowhere. Every source I can find says it's getting bigger.'

Truby responded with a thoughtful nod. Then, decisively, he said, 'OK, this is one for *Pisces*, I think. We need enough space to evacuate a pleasure boat, if that's what it turns out to be.'

'Highly unlikely,' Dietz said. 'Professional tourist boats, fishermen – they know what they're doing. They don't go out in weather like this.'

'Maybe it's a transatlantic yachtsman?' Ben suggested.

Dietz gave a firm shake of his head. 'Any good sailor knows you don't make the crossing at this time of year. It's cyclone season.'

'Whatever we're dealing with, *Pisces* will be able to cope,' Truby said. 'Tim, call Lola; you three had better get going. Addison, you saved the day last time. You want to lead on this?'

Tim and Addison rose to their feet. Addison's face was serious but flushed with excitement. Caroline said quietly, 'Jason, I'd like to go with them.'

Truby hesitated for a second. He was about to answer when Ben interrupted. 'Can I go too, please? I was handy at the ANPECO rescue, right?'

'It's *Pisces*,' Tim said. 'They can just observe. They'll be fine, Jason.'

'I'll be coming along to help,' Caroline said. 'Just so we're clear there's to be no argument. I've already observed enough, these past weeks. It's about time I joined in.'

Truby eyed her keenly. 'You sure you're ready? I didn't really imagine that an aquatic rescue would be your first.'

'I'm an excellent diver and also a fairly expert sailor, Jason.'

'Of course you are,' he replied with a dry chuckle. 'You fancy types, with all the sports.'

Ben didn't say anything for a few minutes. His mother would be going out into high winds and treacherous waters, possibly even risking her life. He felt a vague sense of unease that he'd never experienced while watching her scale a mountain.

'I'd still like to go,' he said. 'Can I? I won't get in your way.'

Caroline nodded. 'Very well, Ben. But remember, on *Pisces*, Tim is the skipper. You do exactly what he says.'

'Aye aye, Ma.'

Walking to the *Pisces* launch pod, Ben felt a thrill of pride and anticipation as he watched Caroline, Lola, Tim and Addison slipping into their Gemini Force jackets. All five lined up outside the doors to the exit gate, which was a lift.

The descent took almost a minute. *Pisces* was obviously at a lower level than the aeroplane hangar pods. When the doors opened, the crew walked into a small antechamber. There was no sign of *Pisces*. Three of the four walls were covered with pegs from which hung controllable buoyancy jackets, helmets, octopus air sources and masks. Ben watched as Tim, Addison, Lola and Caroline kitted up with jackets and masks. The helmets and watertight respirators, they carried. Ben noticed that the respirators looked different from the type that had been used in the firefighting situation.

Once they were ready, Tim touched a panel in the fourth wall. A circular section of the floor about a metre in diameter first sank by thirty centimetres and then rolled steadily to one side. Tim led them all to the narrow spiral staircase beneath. Once they'd all descended, Ben realised they must be inside *Pisces*. He felt a vague pang of annoyance that he hadn't been able to see the whole craft from outside.

In here, the corridors were narrow, greenish-grey and metallic. Ben followed the crew through the main passenger chamber. Rows of narrow metal bench-seats with cushioned backs and safety harnesses occupied most of the available space. *Pisces* had none of the luxurious ambience of Gemini Force One. It was more claustrophobic, stark and utilitarian. But it could shift – at a top speed of forty-five knots, it was as fast as a powerboat.

Beyond the main chamber – which Ben assumed was to house evacuated passengers – and towards the ship's bow was the pilot command centre. It included an array of eight screens – each displaying different information – two banks of tall computer servers and just two seats. Tim was already running through the launch checklist with Addison.

Lola smiled at Ben and Caroline. 'Pretty impressive, huh? But we'd better get out of their way.' She lowered her voice so that only Ben could hear. 'It's Tim's first lead. We've never had *Pisces* as the main rescue vessel before. He's bound to be a little nervous.'

She led Ben and Caroline back to the passenger chamber. They took seats in the front row. Lola activated a screen that was suspended from the ceiling, slightly ahead of them. It displayed one of the satellite maps showing the weather in the Caribbean.

Ben stared. Those cloud systems looked wild.

⟁ BELOW ⟁

Fifty metres below the surface of the Caribbean Sea, there was little indication of the turmoil above. But Ben soon felt the difference as *Pisces* began to surface.

Peering out of a window, he saw bleak depths to the sky. Its greyness was reflected in the rolling ocean. Enormous, breaking crests and flying spray reduced visibility to almost nothing.

They'd reached the storm. Ben could already feel it in his stomach and guts, which lurched with every pitch of the boat. He was lucky in being relatively immune to the worst effects of seasickness, such as dizziness and vomiting. Just the same, it wasn't a comfortable experience.

Lola pointed to the screen above. She explained that it now showed periscope data being mapped onto sonar data. The resultant image was an animation of the projected position of the source of the distress signal.

It was a catamaran. According to visual and sonar data, it had capsized. Two hulls were occasionally visible above the waves, thanks to two bright white stripes of anti-fouling paint. The rudders on each side of the boat were the highest points visible. At first glance Ben thought the rudders were two people standing on the twin hulls of the capsized catamaran. Until it dawned on him that they weren't moving.

If there were survivors, they'd be beneath the water now.

The distress radio beacon was still sending, but no one had heard from them via audio. There was a chance that there was no one left alive, but at least Gemini Force had found them.

Ben followed Caroline and Lola to the command centre. The tension aboard had noticeably shifted up a notch. What awaited them inside the boat – desperate survivors on their last mouthfuls of air? Or just dead bodies?

He grasped a handhold as the boat tipped upwards and then slammed down again. The waves were at least twelve metres high. Now that they'd surfaced, the crew experienced every swoop and drop.

Addison handed a loop of rope to Caroline, who immediately knotted it around her waist. Then the two women kitted themselves out in inflatable life jackets, diving masks with small gas cylinders that attached at the waist, and helmets. With each violent motion of the waves, they staggered.

In exasperation, Addison yelled out, 'Next time let's get kitted up before you bring the boat to the top!'

Then they tested their video and audio transmissions. When they were satisfied that everything was working, Addison asked Tim if anything had been heard from inside the boat.

'Not a peep,' he said, shortly.

Caroline and Addison acknowledged this with simple nods. Ben guessed they were disappointed. There certainly weren't any other rescue agencies anywhere close. Gemini Force had responded at light speed, relatively. All the same, it was disheartening to think they'd come all this way for no more than a body recovery.

'I'm as close as I can safely get without risking a crash,' Tim said. 'We're pitching about like crazy here. There's a lifeboat moored to our inner hull. I'm going to rotate that section of the hull to expose it. Get across and see if you can climb on board. Then hitch a safety line between *Pisces* and the cat. Use the rudder – it looks sturdy enough. And take care! It's a force-ten gale out there. The water's going to be churning like guts after ten pints and a curry.'

Ben watched Caroline and Addison make their way to the upper deck. He barely caught his mother's eye long enough to make a hopeful gesture of good luck. Then they were gone. Lola, Tim and Ben turned their attention to the screens. Two were now showing the video feeds from Addison and Caroline's helmet cams.

Caroline quickly located the lifeboat, an orange fibreglass dinghy that looked large enough to hold six people. A small motor engine was located at the rear. Once inside, she and Addison launched the craft, heading away from the side of *Pisces*. Ben's attention switched from Caroline's to Addison's feed, watching his mother in action, running the safety line from where she'd fastened it to the deck of *Pisces* while Addison steered the boat.

The dinghy took seconds to reach the side of the capsized catamaran. He watched Caroline secure the safety line to one of the upturned rudders, which were almost as tall as she was. The hull of the lifeboat rose and fell with crazy abandon as each wave lifted and then dropped it. He saw Caroline and Addison dive into the foaming water. The screens turned a deep teal colour as they swam underwater. Then the helmet cameras switched automatically to infrared, turning everything to grainy black and white.

Caroline turned herself upside down for a few seconds. Her air bubbles floated past the helmet cam. Ben guessed that she was trying to better orient herself on the capsized boat. Now, on-screen, they saw the dimly lit images of a shadowy deck.

Ben could just make out the different parts of the catamaran. He tried to locate the mast. It took a while for him to realise – all that remained of the mast was a stump at right angles to the broken tip. A sail flapped towards Caroline. She ducked just in time to avoid the boom as the water current swung it across the transom, just behind the cockpit. She grabbed hold of something and pulled herself deeper underwater.

Addison appeared, viewed by Caroline. She was already at the door of the cockpit. Caroline stopped, her helmet pressed up against the glass of the saloon.

Through the glass, they could see three pairs of legs.

They were clearly firmly planted. The rest of the bodies were not visible through the water due to the angle of the window, but the legs weren't floating.

Three people. *Alive.*

Inside the saloon, the water must have been deep because its surface wasn't visible through the glass. Ben guessed that it was at least up to the survivors' chests. He knew they would be cold, their core temperatures dropping fast, in danger of hypothermia. In any waters less forgivingly warm than the Caribbean, they might already be dead.

Addison had turned herself upside down now, so that she could brace both feet on the upper deck. She was pushing at the door. Inside, a face appeared suddenly. It was a dark-haired, bearded man, somewhere between thirty and forty years old. The water level inside the saloon reached the base of his neck. The survivor's eyes were a wild mixture of panic and relief. He was making hand signals to Addison. The door was the only thing keeping the water out of the cockpit.

Next to Ben, Lola shifted uncomfortably. 'They won't have long to get them out of there.'

Addison seemed to have persuaded the bearded man to stop holding on to the door. The bearded face had now been joined by another – a white Hispanic woman of a similar age to her crew-mate. The woman touched her fingers to the glass as if to reach out to the rescuers. Slowly, relief was beginning to register on their faces. Ben had to remind himself that their heads would be trapped somewhere close to the floor of the catamaran's cockpit.

Addison pushed open the door and Caroline instantly launched herself inside, smooth as a torpedo. She swam directly for the survivor who was furthest away. It was a clean-shaven young man, who looked to be in his twenties. He'd been jammed between the bottom of a countertop and the floor, with cushions to hold him in place above the water line. His head and right hand were bandaged in a makeshift fashion. Both bandages were heavily blood-stained. Like the other two survivors, he wore a life jacket but, unlike theirs, his wasn't inflated.

'We've got one pretty severe-looking head injury,' Caroline said. Her voice echoed around the submarine's pilot command centre. 'I'm going to give this man my breathing apparatus. He's not conscious enough to hold his breath up to the surface.' She checked his life jacket. 'Life jacket emergency inflator is already activated. It must have failed. We're going to need to take these people out one by one.'

Caroline pulled off her diving mask and arranged it over the young man's head. He looked half-dead. His eyes were flat, barely acknowledging her presence.

'No time to do it one by one,' Addison said. 'Water levels are rising too fast. I'll take the kid. One of the other survivors can help me.' Ben watched Addison explain this to Caroline through gestures – and then saw his mother hand over the limp body of the injured man to Addison. Addi and the male survivor steadied him between them, then pushed off, swam through the open door and into the swirling blue ocean beyond.

Ben realised that he'd been holding his breath. His heart was thudding, his knuckles white as his fingers curled tightly around the hand rails inside *Pisces*. Watching the rescue at such close quarters was almost like being there. Except that he wasn't. In the end, he was nothing more than a helpless bystander.

And, up on the twin screens, Addison and Caroline were about to save three lives.

⌐ BLOCKED ⌐

A capsized catamaran does not sink. It has no heavy keel. Compartments within the twin hulls trap air inside. Even in heavy seas, it will float.

Ben had sailed on such a boat, many times. His father had been the expert sailor, but Ben and his mother had learned fast. A boat that had taken on so much water inside the cockpit had to be somehow flawed, he realised.

As she swam over the upturned deck, Addison's helmet camera pointed straight ahead. Ben noticed that a crack ran along the join between the hull and the bridge deck. The boat was flexing badly. When he switched to his mother's helmet view he could see that, with each wave, a spurt of water rushed through the crack and into the saloon.

The air pocket was shrinking. With three people breathing from that pocket, the carbon dioxide levels would have risen. No wonder the injured guy had passed out. Without a diving mask Caroline and the final survivor wouldn't last long either.

Ben began to feel an itching, crawling sensation — rising, unbearable tension.

Why weren't they leaving?

Inside the main saloon, the water level was noticeably closer to the helmet camera. He guessed that it would now reach Caroline's chin. She'd given her diving mask to the injured sailor. Once the water reached Caroline's mouth, the game was all but over.

There was just about enough time to calm the final survivor. They'd need to take deep breaths and swim out of there to the safety line.

Why weren't they leaving?

Ben heard the sound of his mother drawing a huge breath, then her head dipped below the water level. He released the breath he'd been holding.

Finally.

He tore his attention away from Caroline's video feed to watch Addison's progress. She'd resurfaced now, along with the two survivors. They were making slow progress along the side of one of the hulls, clinging to the safety line. At the end of the rope and moored to the rudder, the lifeboat was wallowing in huge waves.

Addison would have to get the two survivors higher, on top of the upturned hull, or else risk being struck by the violent motion of the lifeboat. Without helmets, such a blow would mean certain death.

Ben threw a glance across to Tim. Inside the pilot command centre, he was mesmerised by the images on the video screen. He seemed pensive, preoccupied. Too nervous to speak.

There was nothing they could do. Tim had to remain at the helm, using the engines to correct the sea's every attempt to drag *Pisces* away. Lola was preparing the medical room. Minutes from now, the injured survivor would be counting on her to treat his wounded head.

Ben was starting to think that he should have insisted they let him join in. Ben's own PADI diving certification was low-level, but he wasn't completely useless in a diving suit. Unlike here on *Pisces*, where he could do nothing but watch.

The thought rekindled his anxiety. His eyes went back to Caroline's video feed. It took a few seconds to comprehend what he was seeing. His mother's hands were directly in front of the helmet camera. They were struggling to push something back. Then he saw clearly – the female survivor's feet were kicking out, pushing Caroline away. The woman was underwater, intentionally so, her hands reaching for something. Abruptly, Caroline's hands gave way. The soles of the woman's deck shoes lunged at the camera. The angle changed. It was now skewed.

The woman had kicked Caroline's helmet. It still moved with his mother's body, but at a strange angle. He saw the fingers of Caroline's left hand reaching to readjust the helmet but, from beneath the water, a fist lunged. His mother swayed in the water. She rose to the surface.

The final survivor emerged, her mouth twisting in angry, staccato movements.

'The audio's gone!' Tim said. 'She must have knocked out the mic. What the hell's going on in there?'

It was a relief to hear Tim's frustration. Ben felt exactly the same, but he was afraid to criticise.

Tim pointed. 'The woman doesn't want to go. Look. She's pushing your mother away. She's trying to save something. Whatever it is, it's underwater.'

Ben froze. The water level had risen still more. The woman, having thrust Caroline to one side, had taken a breath. Now she was underwater. Caroline followed her. This time he saw that the woman was tugging a door to what looked like a tall refrigerator. With a final, wild glare at Caroline, she yanked the door open.

Stacks and stacks of neatly bundled rolls of bills cascaded out of the open refrigerator. They tumbled and floated chaotically in the water.

A roll passed within centimetres of the helmet camera. They were fifty-dollar bills. Dozens of tightly wound rolls. Hundreds of thousands of dollars.

'Jeez – no!' Tim's cry shot through Ben. 'They're a bunch of skanky drug dealers!'

'Drug dealers …?' Ben repeated.

Tim's hands moved rapidly across a touchscreen. 'They're bringing back *money*. No wonder they risked crossing in such mentally stupid weather conditions. I should have suspected. *Clueless* drug dealers, pulling an imbecile manoeuvre like that.'

Ben didn't reply. He couldn't take his eyes off the screen. The female survivor's hands were sweeping the water inside the main saloon, snatching up rolls of cash and stashing them inside her jacket. Every time Caroline tried to stop her, the woman shoved his mother aside.

Underneath his feet, *Pisces* rose suddenly, lifted at least twenty metres.

'That's gonna be a big one … hold tight!' Tim yelled.

Ben managed to hang on as, abruptly, the floor dropped away. For a second he hung in mid-air. Then he was slammed back against the deck as the submarine slapped against the bottom of the wave.

A rogue wave, maybe twenty metres high. The capsized catamaran would be next. Ben could scarcely bear to watch. If it finally tore the catamaran apart, his mother would have to take her chances. At least she still had a safety line and a helmet.

Caroline's helmet camera was relaying utter mayhem. Water swirled and whooshed before the lens, stirring up a soup of dollar bills.

'Get the hell out of there, you *stupid* dope-slinging cow!' Tim screamed.

Ben wanted to scream, too, but what was unfolding before his eyes was too compelling.

As the maelstrom of water cleared, Caroline once again dived beneath the surface. Now he saw what she saw. That last wave had stirred things up. The refrigerator had fallen over. It was lying flat on its side. Caroline rushed towards it. He could see her hands in front of the helmet camera.

'What's she doing?' Ben asked.

Tim's eyes flicked in Ben's direction and then back to the screen. He turned white.

Ben felt a tide of panic swell inside his chest. It exploded.

'She's trying to shift the fridge!'

'Ben...'

'She's...'

A terrible calm flooded him. He turned to Tim, saw the vacant, horrified look in the pilot's eyes.

Cold with dread, Ben said, 'The fridge is blocking their only way out of there, isn't it?'

Dumbstruck, Tim nodded.

Ben launched himself along the swaying deck. He was heading for the equipment closet, near the medical room. A few seconds later his hands were fumbling with a diving mask and a helmet. 'Let me go over there!'

'Ben.' Lola emerged from the medical room. Her hand touched his shoulder. Her eyes glistened. 'You can't go. None of us can. We wouldn't reach her in time. You've got to leave it to Addison.'

The words were torn from him, a wail of helpless despair as he and Lola headed back to the cockpit. 'Addi, get back down there! My mum's going to drown!'

On the other video feed, they could all see that Addison was in the process of guiding the two survivors into the lifeboat. It would be precious minutes before she could safely leave them.

'Addison.' Tim's voice was firm, insistent. 'Addison.

The instant you've got them safely into the lifeboat, go back down there.'

'Something wrong back there?' Addison asked. 'Where's Ceecee?'

'They're drug dealers, Addison. The one inside the boat tried to save their cash. It was inside the fridge. It looks like the wave just pulled the fridge over. I think it may be blocking Caroline's way out.'

'It *is* blocking their way out,' Ben cried. 'You've got to go back and help! Mum's trying to move the fridge. I don't think she's going to be able to do it!'

Suddenly, Addison was moving at double speed. She shoved the final survivor ahead of her and practically dumped him headfirst into the lifeboat. Then she turned and dived back into the waves.

Inside the main saloon, Caroline had come up for air. The helmet camera was touching the floor of the cockpit now. Ben could see that there were probably only centimetres of air left. She took another gulp and then plunged underwater again, pulling at the fridge door. It barely budged.

Ben began to tremble. 'No,' he murmured, low and frightened. He felt small and vulnerable. His mother was going to leave him for ever. 'Please. Please. Not this. Not this.'

Tim risked a quick glance and then gave a nod to Lola. A second later she was beside Ben, touching his hand.

'Ben. Be strong. Addison's going to do what she can.'

'You've got to get down there with something to smash the glass!' he raged. 'Or blow open the door! Don't expect me to just stand here watching! Let me go over there!'

Tim and Lola didn't move. Addison had reached the cockpit now. She was upside down, her feet braced against the upper deck, her hands fighting with the door. But the fridge had jammed it firmly into place. On the other side of the glass, they could see the two women inside the main saloon, Caroline and the survivor, struggling to move the fridge.

One after the other, they floated back to the air pocket. It had to be minuscule now.

This time, only Caroline returned.

'Come back and help her, you cowardly, greedy ...' Ben's tirade ended with a desperate sob.

The final moments ticked away. His mother was using the last of her energy to fight but it wasn't going to be enough. Caroline released the fridge, floated closer to the door. Addison rotated in the water until she was right side up. They stared at each other through the glass. For a few seconds, the two women made a silent connection.

Slowly, with large, calm eyes Caroline mouthed, very clearly, 'Ben, I love you.'

For a second, Ben couldn't breathe.

Then he blurted, 'I love you too, Mum, don't give up! Addison, tell her!'

On his mother's video feed, they watched Addison saying, 'Ben loves you.'

Caroline looked sad. There was the ghost of a smile. Then she shook her head and mouthed, 'Don't watch.'

She turned away. She floated to the surface. The helmet camera was against the floor again. This time it was touching water.

Addison began to beat her hands against the door. She kicked and punched, slow motion, ineffectual gestures of rage.

Tim and Lola faced Ben. Tim took a step to the side, blocking Ben's view of the screen. 'Listen to your mum,' he said, gently. 'Don't watch.'

◄ DROWN ►

There was a ringing in Ben's ears. It took a while to fade. By the time he could hear what Lola was trying to tell him, he'd noticed that there was a soft red blanket arranged loosely around his shoulders.

He had no memory of how it had got there.

'Drink,' commanded Lola. She was holding a mug of something to his lips. He caught the aroma of rich chocolate. 'You're in shock.'

Ben didn't know what she meant by 'shock'. His nerve endings didn't seem to be responding properly. The next thing he registered was that he was holding the mug. Studying its contents.

She's dead.

The thought was followed by a closing down of his mind. He felt a choking sensation in his throat. A dull ache in his chest. Yet his eyes were dry, like desert pebbles scraping and stinging the sockets of his eyes.

'What's the last thing you heard me say?' Lola asked.

He tried to return Lola's gaze. Tried to turn his mind back. Minutes ago? Or was it hours? Time had become somewhat disconnected. '"Don't watch"?'

'Tim said that, not me. You don't remember anything since then?'

Ben stared into the foam on the hot chocolate. 'I should have watched.'

'She said not to.'

Mouth still dry, he said, 'Mum shouldn't have been alone.'

Lola nodded. 'We all need a companion for our death.'

He swallowed. 'How long until we get back?'

'An hour.'

'What did Tim do with the two survivors?'

'Jason's been talking to the Drug Enforcement Administration. In Florida – that's where they were sailing out of. They're going to rendezvous with us soon.'

'We're going to hand them over?'

'It's the best solution. If we hand them over in Colombia or even Mexico, there's a good chance whoever they work for will get to them. Even in America, to be honest.'

'How much money was in the boat?'

'Hidden in that fridge? About two million dollars, according to the one who's talking to Tim.'

Tonelessly Ben said, 'My mother died saving a couple of drug dealers.'

'The DEA are hoping these two will testify against whoever paid them all that cash. Or the one who sent them.'

'Do you really believe that?'

Lola gave a minimal, helpless shrug.

Ben rose to his feet. They'd left the storm behind.

Yet, walking towards the command centre, he felt as unsteady as ever.

Without a word, he took the co-pilot's seat, turned his attention to what Tim and Addison were doing as they moved around the command centre. They only gave him long, considered looks. Since he didn't appear much in the mood for conversation, they didn't say anything. Occasionally he asked a question about *Pisces*. Tim answered in a voice that seemed entirely detached.

Addison was, for the most part, absolutely silent.

Ben scarcely noticed the rest of the journey. Later, back on Gemini Force One, he found he couldn't remember much of what had happened on the way back.

The atmosphere on the base was icy. A profound silence seemed to have settled. The sounds of the various information feeds into the command centre seemed to have been muted. The crew were sombre. A couple of times, their sorrowful gazes would settle on Ben.

It had only been a few hours since *Pisces'* return but Ben was already getting sick of those looks: pity, sympathy and anxiety. As if he didn't have enough of that for himself.

He sat alone in Caroline's cabin, perched on the end of the lower bunk. In his hand was a photograph of his mother, father and himself. In the photo, Caroline was smiling widely. A world-beating smile.

Someone knocked on the door.

'What is it?' Ben asked flatly.

'A door,' Jasmine said, from the other side. 'And if you open it, maybe I can get in ...'

Ben stood, opened the door and led Jasmine over to a tiny, compact seating area. He took one of the two tub chairs. Jasmine didn't sit. Instead, she regarded him with a mixture of confusion and sadness.

'I was gonna hug you.'

'Oh.' Awkwardly, he stood up again. Jasmine took a couple of steps closer. She opened her arms, squeezed him around the waist and released him.

'Thank you,' he said.

That was what you were supposed to say, wasn't it? When people expressed sympathy? He tried to remember back to when his father had died. Just a few months ago. And yet, somehow, this experience felt entirely new.

'Dude – you look messed up.'

He gave a couple of short nods. 'Yeah. I might be.'

Jasmine dropped into the second tub chair. 'Haven't you cried?'

He looked blank. 'I want to.'

'You can't?'

'I suppose.'

'Want me to leave? Maybe if I do, you'll be able to.'

'I didn't cry when my dad died.'

'OK.' There didn't seem to be much else to say to that. Jasmine waited, patient yet clearly expectant.

'Perhaps there's something wrong with me,' Ben sighed.

'It's OK to cry. It doesn't make you weak. Addison's

the toughest person I've met and she's crying. I saw her go off to *Aquarius* pod. Tears were rolling down her cheeks.'

All Ben said was, 'Oh.'

Jasmine gave him a thoughtful look. 'What are you feeling, right now?'

He shrugged. 'Hard to say.'

'You're feeling *something*, yes?'

Another shrug. There didn't seem to be any easy way to put his feelings into words. He couldn't think of any words that could begin to express what he was thinking and feeling.

All the same, he tried. 'I feel ... pretty awful.'

'You're being too English about it. What has your Austrian side got to say?' Jasmine demanded.

Ben shook his head, slow and deliberate. '*Keine Ahnung.*' No idea.

But his calmness masked an interior chaos.

They were interrupted by the arrival of Truby. He knocked only once, then let himself in. With only the smallest gesture at Jasmine, he seemed to dismiss her.

Ben stood automatically, falling back on his training from school to stand whenever a teacher entered the room.

Truby's eyes were on his, hooded and dark with concern.

'Ben, sit down.' Then Truby sat. He seemed to consider his next words with great care. 'There are horrible things in life. Like what happened to

Carrington. Like this. Sometimes, they just happen. It's really, really important not to take it personally.'

Finally, Ben found his voice. 'No. They don't *just happen*. My mum died because a lowlife drug dealer was trying to get her score back to the even lower-life that she worked for.'

'Or because a fly-by-night rescue agency sent her out on a mission. Or maybe because she met a bonehead, name of Jason Truby.'

'No.'

Truby sighed. 'When you lose a person you love in a freak accident, it makes sense to look for someone to blame. That's what you're doing, Ben. Suddenly you're trying to find a pattern in the universe – like you were *singled out* for misery.'

'I guess.'

'It won't help. Trust me – I know.'

Ben's shoulders slumped. 'If you say so.'

'Maybe it's better to take another attitude. The one people take when they, or people they love, are *saved* by some kind of miraculous intervention.'

'What d'you mean?'

Truby's reply was careful, deliberate. 'You might be surprised how much people take miracles for granted. They don't give it more than a couple of days' thought. We rescue people and they go back to their lives. They're grateful, sure. But they just accept it.'

Ben shrugged. 'OK.'

'There is no Fate, only randomness. But once in a

while, we get to intervene. Quiet miracles. That's what we're about, here, kid. We saved two people today.'

'Scumbags,' Ben muttered, 'who probably deserved to die. My mum didn't.'

'No, she didn't.'

Stubbornly, Ben shook his head. There were tears in his eyes. 'Her death *can't* be meaningless. I won't let it.'

Deliberately, Truby said, 'What exactly can you do about it?'

For a moment, Ben studied Truby. The man seemed placid, calm. If he felt anything at all, it was buried deep. 'I don't get it. I thought you … and my mum … I thought …'

'I cared a *great* deal about Caroline, Ben.'

Ben could only stare.

Truby gave a slight nod. 'It's true. I hadn't told her yet; I was giving her time. Now she's gone and I'll never be able to tell her. But here on GF One, we're going to keep going about our business. The performing of quiet miracles. I think your mom would like that, don't you?'

Ben watched Truby leave the room, baffled. He didn't know what he'd expected from the man. Some words of comfort, at least. Instead, it felt as though Truby was issuing a challenge: *'What exactly can you do about it?'*

Ben had hoped for some relief from the profound loneliness he was experiencing now. Truby *said* he'd cared about Caroline. So why wasn't he devastated? It was as though there was something cold and unreachable about him. As though he'd long ago been hollowed out.

Had Truby filled that void with Gemini Force?

Ben wiped a solitary tear from his cheek. If only he could do the same.

QUIET MIRACLES

'*Quiet miracles*? He said something similar after Gary Lincoln died. I guess this tragedy is making him get a little philosophical. Truby can be a tough one to read. He doesn't give too much away.'

Toru moved steadily through a series of bicep curls with two ten-kilo weights. He stared directly ahead into the mirrored wall of the gym. The pilot's taut, sculpted arms and shoulders were obviously the result of regular weight work.

Next to him, Ben picked up a ten-kilo dumb-bell. 'Who's Gary Lincoln?'

'He was the pilot of *Leo* before me.'

'And?'

'And he died. Road traffic accident, in Mexico. He liked to drive fast.'

'He didn't even die in action?'

Toru shook his head. 'That's the irony.' There was something oddly detached about Toru's manner – as though he regretted bringing Gary Lincoln up and now wished to push the whole memory away.

'Was he reckless?' Ben asked.

Toru replied slowly. 'Maybe. There were no witnesses. There was probably another car involved, but we'll never know for sure. Dumb stuff happens, man. We're not immune, even in Gemini Force.'

Ben began lifting the dumb-bell with his left arm. Toru's voice and entire tone had changed as he talked about Gary Lincoln. It wasn't something Ben could put his finger on exactly, but there'd been a definite shift in the emotional landscape. Still, wrapped up as he was in his own misery, Ben didn't pursue the question any further.

Being shut up inside the guest cabin last night had quickly become unbearable. Unable to sleep, Ben had taken Rigel and a blanket, in the middle of the night, and gone to lie down in the Marina room. The flow of the water and the luminescence of the turquoise pool had helped to soothe him to sleep. None of the adults had been able to find him to offer their shoulder to cry on. Most of all, Rigel's low, throaty little moans had confirmed to Ben that the dog was missing Caroline, too.

He began to exercise the muscles of his right shoulder and said to Toru, 'So Truby's becoming a philosopher?'

Toru grimaced. 'I suspect he's got some deep stuff going on. Not religious exactly but spiritual, maybe. Losing Gary hit us all pretty hard. Not just me. It wasn't something we'd been through before.'

There it was again – the hint that Gary and Toru had been close. Slowly, a possibility began to dawn on Ben. Had the two been an item?

'You were Japanese Air Force, right? Tim and Paul,

they were both in the military, too. And so was Addi. What about Gary Lincoln?'

'I was in the Japanese Air Self-Defense Force. Gary was US Air Force, like Addi. We met at a NATO training exercise. He already knew Truby. In fact, Gary recruited me,' Toru explained.

'How come your regiments released you before you'd served a tour?' Ben asked curiously.

Toru replied with a tight, humourless smile. 'Truby. He's got connections that can make things like that happen. We're bought and paid for.'

'Like football players?'

'Exactly.'

Ben thought for a moment. '*Quiet miracles*, though. Gemini Force hardly seems *quiet* … I mean, the uniforms, the aeroplanes – those aren't the kinds of things people will ignore.'

Toru shrugged. 'We've done five interventions since we got started in July. So far we've had no mentions in the media. Truby asks the other rescue agencies to take credit and they've been happy to do it.'

He knelt and put his fingers around the bar of a fifty-kilogram dumb-bell. Ben watched him rise to his feet, puffing out his chest. 'Won't be secret for ever, though,' Toru gasped before pushing the dumb-bell into the air above his shoulders.

Ben was fairly surprised that the secret had held even for the few months that Gemini Force had been operational. But then again, so far the rescue work had been limited to private property or the open sea.

He looked around for a forty-kilo dumb-bell. He'd bench-pressed more, but today he couldn't be bothered to push it. Exercising was just a way to distract his mind for an hour. When it was over, though, he felt grief return like a crashing wave. Close behind it was numbness. Every time he felt tears collecting in his eyes, something made Ben take a deep breath and look straight up until all the moisture had soaked back in. A couple of blinks and he'd be presentable.

Every so often he'd catch a whiff of pure, unguarded terror.

Now, he really was alone.

His Aunt Isolde was his sole surviving relative and, as far as Ben knew, named in his mother's will as his legal guardian in the event of Caroline's death. Would he be expected to go and live with her in Vienna? Unlike her sister, Caroline, Isolde had married a guy who was basically penniless – a university lecturer. They lived with their three young children. Ben couldn't imagine how he'd fit in with his aunt's family in their cramped suburban apartment. He'd be in the way, however much they pretended otherwise.

At sixteen he was still a minor by UK law but his aunt would take his wishes into account – his mother had always promised that, whatever his age. So he had three choices: continue at school, move to live with his aunt, or drop out of school and live alone.

Alone. But where?

Once again, his future was completely uncertain.

It was a shock to discover just how much he'd relied on his mother. She'd absorbed so much of the loss of Casper Carrington. Ben had been shielded from most of the impact of that tragedy. Now, he had no idea what would happen, or what to do.

Wills and houses and legal stuff. Who would take care of all that?

Truby was waiting for Ben outside the gym. He took Ben down to the Marina room, which was empty. The flow of the waterfall had been turned down to a mere trickle, a steady drip through the rocks. For the first time, Ben noticed the background sound of rainforest insects. A spicy scent of hibiscus penetrated the air.

Truby stood, contemplating the depths of the pool. His hands were stuck deep in the pockets of his indigo-blue jeans. After a moment of respectful silence, he spoke.

'I wanted to let you know that the coffin has been delivered. We cut into the catamaran and got your mom's body out last night. She's being kept in a cold storage facility on the lowest deck. But now we need you to decide what to do next. Ben – should we cremate her? Or do you want a burial?'

Ben swallowed. He could scarcely believe he was being asked this question. His mother had been alive yesterday. Warm. She'd touched him. He could still remember the lemon-verbena smell of her hand lotion as they'd stood together on the deck of *Pisces*.

Now he was being asked what to do with her cold, dead body. And, supposedly, by a man who had cared for her. Why wasn't Truby falling apart? His mother was tough but even she'd wept when her husband had died.

What was wrong with Truby? What was wrong with *Ben*?

'I … I dunno. Where would we bury her?'

'It's up to you. Maybe you'd like to keep her close?'

'Close to *where*?' Ben asked. There was a helpless note to his voice. Truby didn't reply. For once he didn't seem to have all the answers.

Ben sensed his new responsibilities like a backpack filled with stones. His first instinct was to tear it off, to throw the weight aside and to run away, free and unencumbered. Maybe he could just hand everything over to Aunt Isolde, and escape. Take his money and travel the world, like one of those gap-year backpackers.

Another part of him, though, felt the pull of a new, opposing force. Caroline's final work had been with Gemini Force. She'd believed in it enough to become their first casualty during a rescue.

If they go on like this, Ben thought, *they'll be having to recruit a whole new team within six months.*

'What do you want, Ben?'

'I want to join Gemini Force,' Ben replied simply. 'You've already vetoed that. So I suppose it'll be the army.'

'Your mother really did *not* want you to join up. Both she and Casper wanted you to stay out of the armed services long enough for you to have time to change your mind.'

'I know,' Ben said flatly. 'Mum was straight with me.'

'Well, your aunt is your guardian now. Perhaps you should talk to her.'

Ben thought quickly. 'Can I stay here?'

'Until the end of school vacation, sure,' Truby replied.

'No – I mean really stay. Like for a gap year. I'd go back to sixth form next year, I promise. It's just a year. Please? School would let me have compassionate leave. Or – screw them – I'll go to a different school.'

Truby regarded him evenly, a hint of bemusement behind his eyes. 'Really? And what would you do here?'

'I'd train Rigel. You'd already agreed with Mum that he could stay on the base.'

'I hadn't. She was still trying to persuade me.'

'But eventually you would have said yes.'

'That's true,' Truby sighed. 'Where your mother was concerned, I was agreeing to everything.'

'Then you should do it,' Ben pushed. 'In her memory. Because it's what she would have wanted.'

'I don't think Caroline wanted Rigel to work rescues,' Truby protested.

'I'd have talked her round.'

Truby nodded. His eyes glistened. Were those tears? 'You might have. You're pretty persistent that way. Just like your mom.'

And for some reason, these were the words that unravelled Ben. He felt his knees give way, legs shaking, chest trembling, as grief washed over him. He leaned against the back of a rattan chair as the tears overtook him.

Truby didn't flinch or hesitate. He put both arms around Ben and held him tight. It didn't last long.

After a moment, Ben pushed him away. He wiped his eyes with the back of his hand and sniffed, hard. Then in a strong, level voice he said, 'I'm sorry.'

Truby tried to smile. 'There are gonna be moments like that. Don't be afraid of 'em.'

'Let me stay. I want to remember her, *here*,' Ben insisted.

'Well, you sure are a chip off the old block,' Truby said. 'I guess that means you'd better stay.'

HIGHER PURPOSE

'It's cool that he's letting you both stay,' Jasmine said, taking a moment to pet Rigel. The dog had been quietly nuzzling Ben's knees with a damp nose, hoping for some affection, but Ben was vague and distracted.

He passed Jasmine a stack of neatly folded T-shirts and a pair of jeans, which she slotted into a section of her cabin-sized pink-and-grey suitcase. She was right – Truby's about-turn in the matter of Ben staying longer at Gemini Force One was pretty cheering.

'Who knows how long it'll last?' Ben responded.

Jasmine zipped up the suitcase and gave him a sympathetic grin. 'Better make the most of it.'

'I will. I'm going to work on making myself indispensable.'

'Then learn to cook,' Jasmine advised.

'Yeah.' He managed a wan smile. 'I already make an epic sandwich – roast chicken, thin-sliced meatballs, sliced tomato, a thin layer of mustard-mayo and just a little bit of rocket.'

'Sounds good. And staying here definitely beats going back to school.'

'I don't think I'd do very well at school, right now.'

'What will you do?'

'Rigel and I are coming with you to Cancun. After we've dropped you at the airport, we'll head back to Cozumel so that I can give Rigel a few proper walks. Then it's back here to show Jason what the pooch can do.'

'He can do stuff?'

'Yeah, I was working with him back home when Mum was setting up the Caroliners. He has this computerised collar that lets him vocalise — like, telling me if someone is still breathing, if he's found survivors, and so on. The idea is that he can go on ahead, or down holes or whatever, and scout out people that we might not be able to find. And, for them, just seeing a dog can help. Seriously, it raises the spirits no end. That's a big part of survival — not giving up hope.'

'I have to say, I'm impressed. If anything happened to my dad or mom, I think I'd want to crawl into a tight little bundle and cry.'

Ben's voice dropped. 'I *do* feel like that, sometimes. I'm not going to lie — it's rubbish — but I want to feel useful, Jasmine.'

Jasmine stepped around the crowded little cabin and gave Ben a long hug. Rigel whined slightly. He only stopped when Ben extended a hand to include him in the embrace. Then his tail wagged hard and he poked his muzzle between the two humans, snorting happily.

After a second or two, Ben allowed himself to enjoy the warmth of Jasmine's affection. Her light brown hair reached her waist and brushed against his wrists. He found himself wishing that she didn't have to leave. With the others, he felt the need to tough things out a bit more. But Jasmine was surprisingly easy company. With her, it was easier to be his unguarded self.

They made their way to the helo-deck. The doors to the Sikorsky S-76 were open. Truby was already in the pilot's seat, sunglasses pushed back on his forehead. Ben picked up Jasmine's suitcase. He led Rigel inside the S-76 and clipped a lead onto the dog's collar. Dietz arrived a few seconds later to say goodbye to his daughter. They made their farewells, then Jasmine joined Ben and Rigel inside the passenger cabin.

The helipad section of Gemini Force One was already beginning its rise to the surface of the sea when Dietz reappeared. He was waving both hands, an expression of intense alarm on his face. The helipad stopped moving upwards. Truby opened the helicopter pilot's door.

Dietz told him, 'We're getting reports of an explosion in the Paramo oil field.'

'ANPECO again?' Truby sounded intrigued.

Dietz gave a nod. 'Maybe.'

'I think they operate a big rig out there,' Truby said thoughtfully.

Over the loudspeakers, James Winch's voice sounded. 'Gemini Force, all members report to command centre. We have a suspected situation in the Gulf of Mexico. Numerous reports from emergency frequencies and social media concerning the Horizon Alpha oil platform.'

Within seconds, Truby had disembarked and was

telling Dietz, 'Listen, I can't leave right now. The kids will have to stay a little while longer.'

'Could one of the others take Jasmine?' Dietz asked.

'Sorry, not until we know more. I can't spare anyone yet.'

Dietz simply stared. 'Are you sure, Jason? Don't you think maybe we all need a few days after Caroline? Maybe we should sit this one out.'

Truby turned to Ben. There was granite in his gaze. 'What do you say, Ben? Should we take a few days to think about Caroline?'

Ben was silent for a moment. Then, 'An oil platform exploding ... that could be pretty bad, couldn't it?'

'Could be just some escaped gas. A fire, maybe. On the other hand, it could be worse. A lot worse. There are hundreds of thousands of barrels of oil in that field. If that stuff keeps pumping, feeding a fire, spilling into the Gulf ...' Truby took a breath, clenched his jaw tight. 'You're pretty much looking at hell on earth.'

'If my mother were here, what would you do?' Ben asked him.

'Ben,' Dietz said, gently, 'that's not the issue. We can't solve all the world's problems from here. Sometimes people are not in the best shape to help.'

Still Truby stared at Ben. 'What's the verdict, kid?'

'Jason! You *cannot* put this on him.'

Truby shot Michael Dietz a long, steely look. 'There is a mission here, Dietz. A higher purpose. We all serve that purpose. Don't we, Ben?'

Ben thought quickly. It didn't seem possible that Truby was actually going to let him, a sixteen-year-old newcomer, take the decision as to whether they delayed mounting a rescue effort – but he was. He became aware of the two adult men, as well as Jasmine, studying him.

They were waiting.

Haltingly, he said, 'Mum would have wanted to get on with it. She never held back. Not when she saw someone in danger.'

Truby nodded, clearly approving. 'Excellent.'

Dietz didn't agree. 'We're not machines, Jason. Addison's badly shaken. The boy should be with his family. And you. Don't tell me you're not affected.'

'Of course I'm affected!' Truby yelled. The sudden force of his distress sent a jolt through all three of them. 'But that doesn't change anything. Those people still need help.'

There was something strangely magnificent about Truby's determination. From the moment Ben had given the go-ahead, he had felt that it was the right thing to do. He could already feel adrenaline surging into his system. As it coursed through him, sad thoughts, lonely thoughts and sorrow were pushed aside. He felt whole again.

OK, so maybe it wasn't a *normal* response. Maybe none of them on the base were normal. But at least they could be useful. What use was sitting around, moping?

'I'm simply sounding a note of caution, Jason,' Dietz sighed. 'That's what you pay me for.'

'I know, Dietz, that's why I'm asking the boy. His mom. His right to have a say. Ben – stay or go?'

Breathing rapidly, Ben looked from Jasmine to Rigel to Truby.

'Stay. Stay and help.'

Truby placed a firm, reassuring palm on Ben's shoulder. He held it there long enough for Ben to experience a swell of pride – and just a small twinge of fear. It was unnerving, taking a decision that seemed to run against the usual cautious advice.

Just a tiny bit like stepping off the top of the Sky-High Hotel.

HORIZON ALPHA

Ben entered the circular conference room, but cautiously avoided taking one of the twelve seats at the round table. Its significance was unmistakeable: a custom-designed piece of furniture into which the twelve signs of the zodiac had been inlaid, cherry wood contrasting with beech. Instead, he leaned against one of the support posts in the open doorway and listened to James Winch.

As Tim passed him on the way to his designated seat next to the *Pisces* sign, Ben whispered, 'How come we're in the conference room this time?'

Tim's eyes widened for a fraction of a second. 'Because you're in the Premiership now, laddie. This is where we coordinate all our major rescue strategies.'

'So the command centre?' Ben asked.

'That's tactical.'

Ben turned his attention to James's speech. All the screens that hung around the room displayed an animated version of the workings of a deep-water oil platform.

'Horizon Alpha is ANPECO's flagship oil rig – an ultra-deep-water, semi-submersible platform. It can pump oil from the rich oil sands you find up to ten kilometres below sea level. A pipe called a "riser" sinks down from the rig into the sea bed about fifteen hundred metres directly below the platform. Early this morning, gas began to seep into the oil well.'

Ben broke in. 'How?'

James turned to him, as though noticing his presence for the first time. 'The guys at ANPECO still don't know how that happened. There's a structure known as a blowout prevention system – the BOP. The BOP is a large structure – four storeys tall. It sits on the bottom of the sea bed, on top of the well. Any potential for an explosion is contained by the BOP, right down there on the sea bed.

'This morning, the BOP failed. A mixture of hydrocarbons – oil and gas – entered the riser. Once that happens – and I'm going to stress this – *once hydrocarbons enter the riser, there is no way to stop them shooting to the surface.* It is no longer a matter of *if* there is an oil leak at the platform, but *when.*'

No one else seemed inclined to interrupt. Maybe they all understood everything. But Ben didn't care about looking clueless in this instance. No one would be surprised that a kid his age didn't know how an oil platform worked.

He said, bluntly, 'OK, that explains how come the oil is shooting up the riser, but what caused the explosion?'

'There was no way to stop the gas in the oil from flooding the mud–gas separator on the Horizon Alpha,' James replied. 'A huge pool of gas collected on the surface. It poured out all over the rig. There may have been some kind of electrical fault – or something much more worrying – but, somehow, the gas ignited. That's your explosion, ladies and gentlemen – four hours and fifteen minutes ago.'

'Something much more worrying?' Ben said. 'Like what?'

James didn't seem to have heard the question. The screens switched to live footage from the oil rig. Ben saw an enormous black cloud within which bulbous orange flames swelled and exploded. The platform was huge. When Ben finally saw a helicopter coming into view, he was stunned by how tiny it looked against the maelstrom of fire and smoke. It was like a mosquito buzzing around a roaring, angry beast of fire.

Paul said, 'ANPECO have called in the emergency services – which I guess means that they've given up trying to solve the problem themselves.'

James nodded. 'You're right – they've given up. They already tried a bunch of solutions – no go. Horizon Alpha has a reported crew of one hundred and fourteen. At this time, thirty-five men are missing. The rest have managed to evacuate. This situation is still in flux. There is good reason to believe that there will be survivors on the rig, perhaps cut off by fire or water.'

Ben piped up, 'Is the rig sinking? You said it was semi-submersible.'

James turned to him. 'Part of the working rig is below water. Accommodations, however, are mostly above water.' He pointed to the screen. 'The fire is mainly on this side, where the mud–gas separator is housed. The accommodations are here. But look at the derrick – it's tilted.' He took a deep breath. 'I'd say there's a risk that this platform is going to sink. Or worse.'

Ben said, 'You keep saying stuff like that. *More worrying, worse.* Are you suggesting this was no accident?'

'Perhaps I'm being paranoid. The most *likely* thing is that it *is* an accident,' James admitted. 'There've been accidents on deep-water rigs before. It's the riskiest type of oil exploration.'

'Maybe so,' Addison said. 'But twice in two months? All this crap hitting ANPECO?'

Truby interrupted. 'Let's leave the conspiracy theories for now and focus. James, what can we do?'

'I just spoke to the head of offshore exploration for ANPECO. He's coordinating all rescue efforts. Four fire-fighting crews are being sent out there to pump water. They'd certainly appreciate another – so I suggest we send Julia in *Scorpio* with a couple of pumps. Paul may be able to help with strategic blasts using the jetpack suit – but I'd use caution there.'

Truby said, 'OK, *Scorpio* – Julia with Paul and some firefighting equipment.'

James continued, 'The main priority right now is to find those thirty-five missing workers.'

'Sounds like a major evacuation,' Truby remarked. 'Tim, Nina, Lola, how about you take *Pisces* and start looking for survivors?'

All the members of Gemini Force that Truby had

mentioned so far began to study a schedule of orders that appeared on their screens.

'I could go with them,' Ben suggested. 'I'm a PADI Open Water-certified diver.'

Truby dismissed him with barely a glance.

'The real issue,' James continued, 'is going to be stopping all this gas-rich oil from rising to the surface. Right now, it's fuelling the explosion. Even if we manage to put that hellfire out, you're looking at ten thousand gallons of oil spilling into the Gulf *every single hour*. That's one heck of an oil slick! Absolutely catastrophic for the marine environment.'

'Can we cap the well?' Dietz asked.

'That's strictly ANPECO's responsibility.' James glanced at Truby. 'But the time may come when we'll be asked to help.'

Truby said, 'James, any ideas?'

'There are a few ways to do it. From what the head of offshore operations told me, they're working on alternative ways of collecting the oil on the surface.'

Ben stared. 'So they're not going to stop the spill? What about the environment?'

'They're going to try to slow down the flow with a method called "top-killing". Basically, you mix drilling mud with household plastic-based garbage and pump it through the system. If it works, it slows down the flow – ideally, brings it to a complete halt. Meanwhile, they bring ships in to collect the oil on top.'

'Is that going to work?'

James looked doubtful. 'I'm not an expert in offshore drilling. My area of expertise, when I worked in the oil industry, was *on*shore. But I've put some feelers out about top-kill. It's thought of as a long shot. Perhaps there's a ten per cent chance it'll work.'

'Why are ANPECO trying it first?' Addison asked.

'For one thing, they don't have many easy options. The blowout preventer is meant to handle these situations. It failed. Now it's time to find another way to cap the well – but it's many metres underwater.'

Ben stepped closer, examining the nearest overhead screen. It was now showing a sonogram of the sea bed. A tall scaffold-type building followed the straight pipe – the riser – upwards. But then, somewhere above this stack, the riser appeared to be bent at an angle of almost ninety degrees. 'Is that the riser?' he asked James.

James stared at the underwater sonar pictures. His expression went from anxious to disbelieving. 'Look at that! The riser is all twisted up. It's going along the sea bed here ... and up there it's twisting again.'

'It looks like the tracks of a rollercoaster,' Ben observed.

'Exactly. And it's about as easy to cut through – i.e. not!'

'Surely there's some way they can cut through the riser and put a cap on top of it?' Ben asked.

For a second, James fixed Ben with an expression of admiration. 'Good one, Ben. That's exactly what they need to do. But I can think of at least three big problems.'

Truby folded his arms. 'We're listening …'

James held up a finger. 'Number one: the riser is a bit more than fifty centimetres across. The walls are extremely thick. You can't cut through that; you have to shear it. Number two: you can't get a diver or even a sub that far down – the pressure is too high – so everything has to be done by remote control. And three: if you do manage to shear through the riser, you have to cap the well with something pretty mega. Something at least as hefty as the BOP, which is already the size of a small apartment block.'

Ben said, 'Why does it have to be so big?'

'The pressure of the oil coming through the riser is extreme. I'd say you need three, maybe four, valves in whatever you cap it with. Then you could close them, one after the other. That might do it.'

Truby said, 'Dietz, you're in touch with all our suppliers. Do we know anyone who might be able to make a part like that?'

Dietz gave a couple of nods. 'Aquamachine in Tianjen, China. They built the parts of GF One that house the energy plant. They're excellent marine engineers.'

'OK, let's get on to them and see about getting something suitable.'

James looked astonished. 'Jason, a cap like this is a permanent thing. It closes off the oil.'

'That's what we want, isn't it?' Ben demanded.

'Not if you're ANPECO!' James replied. 'I mean, that oil refinery fire has already hurt them pretty badly. And now they're going to lose their Paramo oil well, too?'

'I'm not saying we'd use it, James, just that it might be an idea to check out what it would take to get hold of this thing,' Truby said. 'Maybe Aquamachine even have something we can adapt? No one could get it here faster than Gemini Force. We could send Toru there in *Leo* and have it on site at Paramo ten hours later.'

Ben reeled. '*Leo* can make it to China and back in *ten hours*?'

Toru shrugged. 'More like ten and a half, with the extra weight.'

The conference room began to buzz with energy and focused concentration. Ben watched for a few minutes, fascinated by the slick teamwork, as the members of Gemini Force shared information, plans and schedules. Not a word, nor a second, was wasted. An air of quiet professionalism descended. It was almost physically calming.

Eventually, Ben stepped outside and began to walk downstairs to his mother's cabin. Positive, determined energy. This felt so much better than the despair that had threatened to smother him just an hour or two ago.

If only he could be part of it.

~ HIDING PLACE ~

'OK – ready for some aerial firefighting?'

Truby stood in the opening of the conference room. Nina, Lola and Dietz were all sitting at what Ben assumed were their designated seats: *Libra*, *Virgo*, *Sagittarius*. Paul was over on the other side, studying the screen of a tablet computer that rose out of the table at his touch. Julia was standing, getting ready to leave on her mission.

'Julia, you're going to deliver the water pumps to a nearby platform supply vessel. It's one of two PSVs that recently made deliveries to Horizon Alpha. *PSV-Atlanta* was still close enough to turn around and come back. It's empty so there's a lot of space on deck. It's been picking up survivors in lifeboats.'

Julia zipped up her flight jacket. 'All good. What about Paul?'

Truby handed Julia her helmet and gloves. 'First, drop the extra water pumps at the *Atlanta*. Take a look at Horizon Alpha's helipad. If you think you can make a landing, put Paul down in the firefighting suit. There'll be localised spots of fire that may be blocking exit routes. Paul can get in, extinguish the fire and attach a magnetic beacon to the wall. That way, we alert and direct survivors. Then, Paul, you get out fast. *Scorpio* can keep the general area flame-free. All of you, stay in constant touch via radio.'

Ben hovered close by, listening. Truby and the rest of the crew seemed to have developed the ability to look right through him.

'Kind of annoying, isn't it?'

He turned to find Jasmine at his side. Her arms were folded; she leaned against the kitchenette embedded in the outer wall of the circular room that dominated the lower tier of Gemini Force One's upper deck.

'Might be a good time to try out your sandwich-making skills,' Jasmine said with a nod towards the kitchenette. 'It's about the only way you'll get to join in.'

Ben didn't reply. He was thinking back to those awful moments in *Pisces*, when he'd realised that his mother might be in real danger.

'Gemini Force needs more people,' he said, eventually. 'Think about it. On *Pisces*, if I'd been in the water with Mum …'

'Then it might have been you who …' The dark look in Ben's eyes made Jasmine break off.

Ignoring her ominous warning, he said, 'Where do they keep the kit?'

'Down in the main equipment rooms on level three.'

'Level three? I haven't seen that yet.'

Jasmine glanced around. When she saw that they weren't being observed she said, 'Want me to show you?'

Without another word, Ben followed her downstairs. No one noticed them leave.

A few moments later they were in a part of the base that actually felt like the submarine environment that it was. There was none of the blue-infused light that bathed the upper decks here – just dimly lit corridors and metal doors painted with numbers. The feeling was purely functional.

Next to a wide, garage-style door marked '04' were four doors, each no more than two metres from the other. Jasmine opened one. Inside were metal standing shelves, neatly organised. Ben entered the room and examined the contents. On the top shelf were controllable buoyancy jackets, life vests and octopus air sources. Full wetsuits and flippers were on the shelf below.

'What are you doing?' Jasmine asked.

He turned to her. 'There are thirty-five guys on that ship. They're not all going to be in one place. I'm pretty handy underwater. I could help.'

'There's no way Truby is going to let you get onto that rig.'

Ben began to try on a controllable buoyancy jacket. 'Why not? Because my mum just drowned trying to save a drug dealer? You know what Truby said to me after she died? *What exactly are you going to do about it?* Well, I reckon he owes me the right to decide what I do for myself.'

Gently, Jasmine took him by the elbow. 'This is just crazy talk, right?'

Ben picked up a mask. 'My parents are dead. No one's going to miss me, if anything happens. I'm dispensable. And out there, I could actually *do* something.'

Jasmine was visibly shaken. 'I'd miss you. Jason, too. Can you imagine how he'd feel if anything happened to you?'

But Ben's resolve was only growing stronger. Ignoring her comments, he added an air tank and diving gloves to his collection. 'We can get to the individual pods from this level, right? Or is it the level below?'

'The level below. Ben! You're not serious?'

'Totally. Jasmine, I need you to do something for me. Can you get Rigel? I'm going to need his wearable tech, too. It's on my bunk, in my mum's cabin. Everyone's pretty busy – I doubt they'll notice, but can you try not to make anyone suspicious? Bring them back down here. I'm going to find somewhere to hide on *Scorpio*.'

She hesitated. 'I can't.'

Ben fixed her with an unshaking gaze. 'You're not my boss, or my family. We've only just met, so it's not like you owe me any loyalty, but if you were my friend, I promise you, you'd help me do this. I'm not crazy. People are going to die today, Jasmine. Guys with families who are counting on them. I *know* I can help. I have to do this.' Ben's voice dropped, became imploring. 'Please. Be a mate. Get Rigel. Get the collar.'

'You've got your whole life in front of you, Ben.'

'And this is exactly how I want to spend it.'

As if in a daze, Jasmine moved away. After a second she turned and disappeared up the staircase.

Ben let himself relax. He steadied himself against a shelf and allowed himself a couple of deep, shaky breaths. He was a lot more nervous than he had let Jasmine see.

The entrances to the individual hangar pods for the customised Gemini Force aircraft were on level four. As on level three, numbers were painted on the metal doors. *Scorpio* – Julia's main aircraft – was Gemini Force Three, so he picked the door labelled '03'.

Like every door on Gemini Force One, it was unlocked. For a tiny moment it struck Ben that he might be violating the principle of trust that operated on the base. But, he reasoned, it wasn't like he'd asked Truby directly. Truby hadn't actually said 'no'.

Ben pushed all thoughts of repercussions out of his mind. It wasn't difficult. He only had to imagine a room full of oil-rig workers, cowering somewhere in the depths of Horizon Alpha, trapped and praying for rescue.

Minutes later, he discovered that the upholstered row of seats in the passenger cabin of *Scorpio* lifted up to reveal storage space beneath. He stashed the diving equipment. Then he heard the door open with a metallic clunk and heard Rigel's excited barks as he spotted Ben.

Rigel dashed up to him, tail wagging hard. It was all Ben could do to get the dog to calm down. Jasmine handed him the wearable-tech collar.

'I don't even know why I'm doing this,' she admitted, 'because if you don't come back, it's kind of my fault.'

Ben laid a hand on her shoulder. 'This is all on me, Jazz. I knew I could count on you.'

She tried to smile. 'Just come back, is all.'

Before he could reply, the floor began to move. Ben and Jasmine stared at each other, stunned.

'They've started.'

'You'd better get out.'

'I can't! The door seals as soon as the floor starts to rise.' Jasmine glanced around. There was an equipment carrier in the corner of the hangar. 'I'll hide behind that until you've all left.'

They separated, Ben and Rigel into their hiding places on *Scorpio*, Jasmine to the opposite side of the pod. It continued its smooth rise to the surface.

Inside the cramped darkness beneath the seats, Ben nuzzled against Rigel's ears.

'We're going to help them, old boy. For Mum.'

— TILT —

It wasn't long before the technical details of his plan started to loom in Ben's mind. Ten minutes into the flight he was already wondering how he would actually get onto the rig.

Paul was in *Scorpio*'s passenger cabin with him. Ben hadn't counted on that. He'd assumed that Paul would ride up front with Julia. But no. Ben and Rigel were trapped in the under-seat storage. Rigel's training as a guide dog meant that he could remain calm and still for long periods of time. Ben had no such training.

He'd either have to wait until Paul left in the fire-fighting suit, or else Ben would have to reveal himself first. Chances were that, if he did that, Paul and Julia would yell at him a bit but they wouldn't march him back to Gemini Force One. That would endanger the whole rescue mission.

Instead, Ben was pretty sure they'd let him stick around – and then Ben would be on hand to help. Rigel was already good at listening out for the faint sounds of human survivors. He'd be able to lead Ben straight to anyone that could be saved.

Could he trust Paul and reveal himself? Ben didn't want to take the risk of throwing the pilot off his mission. It would probably annoy him. It would definitely force him to make a tricky decision. Better to wait until the last possible moment. Then maybe Paul would have left already on his own mission and wouldn't be around to see Ben emerge.

Far better for the crew of *Scorpio* to realise what had happened when Ben was already on the platform. Yet the more Ben thought about it, the more anxious he became. It was just too dangerous to go onto Horizon Alpha without a radio. Even in his most confident moments, he could see that. He'd have to grab a radio headset.

They were in the air for about thirty minutes. The noise level noticeably increased. As well as the thrumming of the chopper's own rotors and blades, there was an ominous background roar.

The fire.

Ben began to hear a steady stream of instructions being relayed across the intercom. *Scorpio* descended. He felt the landing skids touch down.

They'd reached Horizon Alpha.

Ben was silent, curled up on his side in a foetal position. Rigel began to whine softly. He could sense Ben's anticipation, could smell a new scent in the close air.

Fear.

A healthy dose of reality began to sink into Ben's psyche. He pushed it to the back of his mind. He allowed himself, for a moment, to dwell on the grim memory of his mother's last seconds of life.

Right now – maybe close by – there were guys at risk of a death like that. If he could save even one, it would be worth it.

He waited until he heard the flare of the jetpack on the firefighting suit as Paul swooshed out of the chopper. Then he threw back the seat above his head.

Rigel leaped out of the storage space. He was closely followed by Ben.

The first thing Ben noticed was the searing blast of heat. It took his eyes a second or two to adjust to the boiling ball of light – the blazing orange of the fire. It filled the sky, fifty metres ahead of *Scorpio*. The sound was thunderous. It was a low, terrifying rumble that rattled his ribs. The sky around them was almost entirely black. Ben's senses filled with the overpowering stench of burning metal and oil.

The second thing he noticed was the insane angle of the central tower – the derrick – on Horizon Alpha. It was almost at a diagonal forty-five degrees. Ben couldn't understand how *Scorpio* had landed – the helipad must be equally tilted. Yet, somehow, the chopper was level.

For a moment, his resolve was shaken. So much heat. Every centimetre of exposed skin stung. In another few minutes, he'd begin to cook.

Then he saw how close the accommodations were. A squat, white block at least three storeys high and maybe eighty metres across began just five metres away. At least half of it was under water.

The fire was consuming everything on the opposite

side of the rig. Blasts of white, churning water were directed on the blaze. They came from four different directions. Clouds of steam hissed wherever the water met the flames. Ben couldn't see them through the smoke, but he guessed that there had to be firefighting boats out there.

He was already wearing the controllable buoyancy jacket. In the few seconds left before *Scorpio* moved on, Ben had to assemble the rest of his gear. Then he saw a hosepipe trailing from the open door. It was sucking water up from the sea below the helipad.

Scorpio was taking on water, getting ready to start dousing the flames from the air. That would give Ben the extra minutes he needed.

He moved fast, snapping the breathing tank, octopus and mask into place. He fitted Rigel with the high-tech collar. Next he found a radio headset, in the same cabinet from which he'd seen Paul take one. Ben fitted the microphone and earpiece.

'We're going for another swim, boy,' Ben murmured as he worked. 'Like the lake, but much shorter and a fair bit choppier. You'll be brilliant.'

The heat intensified. Sweat pooled in Ben's hair, forehead and eyebrows and began to run down his cheeks. He took a second to wipe his eyes, then flicked the power switch on Rigel's collar. He tuned the radio frequency to the one used by Gemini Force.

Ben stood, swaying slightly, on the edge of the chopper. Waves swelled about ten metres below. He checked the line of sight to the nearest door of the accommodation block. It was open to the sea, water sloshing in the corridor about a metre deep. There was no way to walk around to the door. Every surface was on a crazy tilt.

He activated his radio headset.

'*Scorpio*, this is Ben Carrington. Rigel and I are going into Horizon Alpha's accommodation decks, carrying out search and rescue. Please alert *Pisces* to our position. Leaving *Scorpio* ...' He grabbed hold of Rigel's collar and inhaled deeply. 'Now.'

Ben didn't wait for a reply.

The drop to the water was longer than it looked. He and Rigel landed with a heavy smack. Sea water shot up his nose. The water was chilly but not too uncomfortable. The power of the sea was a shock. Ben had sailed and dived in open water, yet it never failed to astonish him how small and feeble even a mildly rough sea could make you feel.

He began the swim to the open door of the apartment decks. In his earpiece he could hear Julia screaming at him but, with the sound of waves in his ears, he couldn't tell what she was saying.

It wouldn't be anything good.

Two minutes of battling the ocean and he was swinging for the door handle. He grabbed hold and reached for Rigel, who'd stuck close by. They waited until a wave slapped the door against the opening. It washed them into the corridor.

The passageway was at a weird angle. The water was

up to Ben's chest. He had to walk with one foot on the corner made by one wall and the ceiling, leaning heavily to the right to keep his head in the air pocket. Rigel paddled, head easily above water. Already the dog was more confident in the element than Ben.

Ben hoped that the wearable tech really was water-proof. It wouldn't work if Rigel was entirely submerged, but so long as he could keep his head on the surface and could bite down on the sensor, he'd be able to send signals to Ben. If that failed, the dog could still bark.

'People trapped,' Ben shouted, using his best command voice. 'Rigel, PEOPLE TRAPPED! FIND! FIND! FIND!'

Rigel barked a few times, pricked up both ears and looked expectantly at Ben. For a couple of seconds, Ben almost panicked. Rigel was staring at him as though he'd never heard the words before. Ben repeated the instructions. Then he remembered the final part ...

'Take Ben! Take Ben! Find, find, find!'

Rigel barked twice more and began to paddle furiously until he'd vanished down the corridor. Ben followed.

Finally, in the earpiece of his radio, he heard Julia. 'Ben, Truby says you come *right* back to *Scorpio* now.'

'Can't do that, Julia. Get on with your mission. Tell *Pisces* my position. We're looking for survivors here.'

The floor gave a sudden lurch to the left. Ben stalled, steadying himself against the walls.

'Ben, turn around now! Get out of there!' Julia insisted.

There was another sickening lurch. Both Ben's arms and legs were now braced against the walls of the corridor. In a slow cartwheel motion, Ben felt himself moving head over heels. His head rushed to meet the water. He took a huge breath.

And then Ben was upside down. Totally submerged.

⟿ BLOWBACK ⟾

Ben rolled over and broke the surface of the water. Terror wasn't far away now. He was staring down the corridor. What used to be the floor was now above his head.

There was an almighty sizzling sound – like some gigantic serpent hissing directly into his ear. He glanced at the open door at the end of the corridor, just in time to see a wall of white steam rushing towards him. He barely had time to grab a breath and duck under the water before it washed over him. Thirty seconds later, he emerged. The steam had gone.

For a few seconds, Ben took stock. Horizon Alpha had capsized. It had gone from tilted to flipped within five minutes. It couldn't be long before the entire structure sank.

He began to shout for Rigel. The dog was nowhere to be seen, had turned a corner to the left. Most dogs, when their owners call for them, won't bark in reply; they'll merely run back to check in on their owner. But Rigel had been trained to reply.

If he could.

When there was no answering bark, Ben felt as though the water around him was turning to ice. He could sense panic hovering close by. He began to breathe slowly, calming himself. And to focus, focus, focus.

The ceiling – now the floor – bobbed beneath him, moving up and down with the motion of the waves. Ben tried to reason with himself.

It's stable enough, for now. You've still got time.

A low, sickening thought was sliding into his mind. What if he was wrong and there were no survivors here? Then Ben's actions would do nothing but draw Gemini Force's attention away from their other efforts. Maybe even from the main mission of finding survivors and getting them to safety.

The thought became relentless. *Get out. Cut your losses. Capsized and sinking is too much of a risk. Call Rigel. Go.*

He waited to exhale.

In his earpiece, he heard Julia's voice. Every minute or two, the same thing – the order to return. But then, across Julia's insistent orders, Ben heard the friendly American voice of the wearable tech. Rigel was biting down on one of the six sensors in the collar flap.

'People alive. People alive.'

Ben began to yell again for Rigel. He screamed at the top of his voice until, finally, the dog began to bark continuously, just as he'd been trained. Short, bright yelps at regular intervals. The dog's own location device.

All thoughts of safety were pushed away. Ben pulled the mask over his face and fitted the octopus mouth-piece. Swimming would be more efficient than sloshing through water of this depth. Ben dived into the water and began to power his way towards Rigel.

His mind was filled once again with that awful vision of his mother trapped inside the catamaran's cockpit. He could barely see anything else. He had no other thought, swimming those corridors towards Rigel's voice, than the idea that he could save someone else from dying like that.

He made one left turn, then another. Rigel appeared. The dog was treading water outside a door. When Ben reached him, he stood. The door was cracked open. He put his shoulder to it but, for some reason, it wouldn't open more than a few centimetres.

He pulled out his mouthpiece and yelled, 'Hello?'

Two voices began immediately to shout back. 'It's not just a dog! There's someone out there!'

'Why is the door stuck?' Ben asked.

From inside, a mid-American-sounding voice replied, 'A filing cabinet got knocked down against it. It's wedged in. We can't shift it. Even capsizing didn't budge it. I can't believe you're really here! How many more of you are there?'

'Just me,' Ben said. 'My dog found you.' His heart was pounding. Another door wedged shut. If two oil men couldn't shift the cabinet from the inside then he wasn't going to be much help. He licked his lips.

Think.

Aloud he muttered, 'There has to be a way.'

It began to dawn on Ben that these men, and possibly

he himself, were moments away from a death almost exactly like his mother's. A dread began to grip him, so deep and terrible that he felt his brain might implode.

'No.' He began to shiver. 'Not like this.'

It took another moment to get hold of himself. The water, Ben noticed, was now above his chin. Without a mask, he'd be in trouble pretty soon.

The men trapped inside wouldn't have anything to help them breathe.

There were minutes to go, if anything.

He began to look around the corridor, hunting for anything that might help.

An explosion. That's what he needed. A small explosion to blow open the door. Just enough blowback to shift the filing cabinet. Where was a bit of C4 when you needed it? Or thermite?

Then he saw it. A fire extinguisher, about twenty metres down the corridor. Dimly, Ben remembered TV programmes he'd seen where people exploded fire extinguishers by shooting bullets into them in the name of science.

Now all he needed was a gun.

'Guys...' Ben pressed his forehead against the side of the corridor.

Mum. If there's some kind of afterlife, help me. Please, please let one of them have a gun.

'Guys...' His voice was barely audible now. He forced himself to speak louder. He could scarcely bring himself to say the words. If they said no, he would be ruined. To

swim away now, leaving these men inside, was unthink-
able. '... Have you got a gun ... of any kind?'

There was a stark pause. Then a different voice replied. 'No.'

Ben's eyes closed. He let out a long breath.

'But I know where you can find one,' the voice continued. 'There's a security locker. It's on the floor below,
two doors down to the left from here.'

Ben could feel his heart sinking. 'Below? That's
underwater.'

'No! I meant a lower deck. But we're upside down
now, right? So it should be above.'

Ben could sense a ray of hope. 'OK. OK, good. How
do I get into the locker?'

'The combination is – listen – zero, five, seventeen,
twenty-one, thirty-two.'

'Zero, five, seventeen, twenty-one, thirty-two.' Ben
repeated it a couple of times. He began to whisper it
under his breath, like a mantra. He couldn't afford to
get even one digit wrong – two lives depended on it.
He grabbed hold of Rigel, supporting him in the water
for a moment so that the dog could rest, ruffling Rigel's
sodden ears.

Backing away, he replaced the octopus mouthpiece,
dropped below the waterline and began to swim. About
thirty metres further down the corridor, he found the
staircase. It was behind a fire door. He had to put his
shoulder hard to the door to open it against the sloshing

water. Eventually it gave way. A wave of water slammed into him, almost knocking him off his feet.

Ben swam into the stairwell. As he gazed upwards, he saw something that made his pulse race.

A survivor, floating on the surface.

He swam upwards. His mask broke the surface of the water near to the top of the door to the next level. He turned to face the floating survivor. What he saw next sent a violent retch through him.

The body had been burned, the flesh melted away until the bones of the jaw and one side of the face were exposed. The rest of the man's face had blistered beyond any recognition. One side of his body was charred black.

Ben heard his own voice cry out. His arms flailed in panic. A moment later he'd managed to scramble through the next fire door and onto the level.

The water was up to his thighs. It must have been largely underwater until the platform had capsized. Now all the water would run down, back to the level he'd just left. That was why the water level downstairs was rising so fast.

And he'd opened the fire door. He'd allowed thousands of gallons to flood the deck where the survivors were trapped.

Ben knew he had to hurry.

Two doors down to the left from here, he reminded himself. *Zero, five, seventeen, twenty-one, thirty-two.*

The door would now be on his right. Ben remembered that there had been three doors between the room with the trapped men inside it and the stairwell. That meant the security locker must be inside the room through the first door to his right.

He grabbed the door handle and found, with relief, that it wasn't locked. He located the locker quickly – a gym-style, upright metal locker with a combination lock. Still breathing the numbers he'd memorised, Ben opened the door.

Inside was a gun, some kind of revolver.

He was back in the stairwell a minute later. Then he was swimming hard in the corridor below. There was almost no air remaining – less than half a metre. Rigel greeted his reappearance with a joyful yelp. As he passed the fire extinguisher, Ben dived deeper and pulled it away from the wall.

The revolver was in his hand, the extinguisher tucked under his left arm. Now he had to find some way to jam the extinguisher into the door crack. Ben tucked the gun through one of the fastenings in his buoyancy jacket. Then he pushed the narrowest part of the fire extinguisher, the nozzle, in through the opening. He kept pushing until he could feel that the neck of the extinguisher was tightly jammed within.

From the room beyond there was silence. Ben guessed the men inside would be as high up as possible, faces turned towards whatever air was left.

Just like his mum.

The mental picture was too grim to contemplate.

Instead, he focused on the sound of his own precious oxygen washing through the mouthpiece.

When the water load became too heavy, the oil platform would sink to the bottom of the ocean. Like a stone. There was no chance anyone would survive that – and it was just a matter of time.

He must be down to the last handful of minutes by now.

Ben removed his mouthpiece and floated to the surface.

'I'm going to shoot now,' he yelled. 'Get away from the door. Try to take cover!'

The two men inside shouted back their agreement as Ben pushed Rigel far behind him. 'Stay!' he shouted. He lowered himself underwater, breathing mask back in place, and drew the weapon.

This was it.

Ben aimed straight at the top of the extinguisher. That had to be the weakest point. The water would dampen any explosive effect but he could only hope it would be enough.

━ CAMZEEN ━

Ben had fired a shotgun before but never a handgun. The kick was harder than he'd expected. He felt the blast of the explosion a millisecond later. A wave of energy threw him back and sideways. He flipped his head to watch the remains of the red canister of the extinguisher shoot past. The water slowed it enough that it missed him by a centimetre.

The door was hidden behind a froth of water and foam. Hands tingling in expectation, he waited. Then he saw something that made his spirit leap.

A face burrowing through the churn. Then another. Both men were free. Their eyes were wild with desperation. They barely seemed to register his hovering presence, a masked boy floating in the flooded corridor. When they broke the surface, they gasped, long and deep.

Ben didn't dare wait another moment. Rigel's paws were level with his eyes now, paddling away as the dog began to struggle to breathe. Ben tugged at the nearest survivor. There wasn't time to talk. He had to lead them all now. Out of this sinking hell-hole.

He checked only once to see if they were following. Rigel was slower now. The men were taking breaths then diving, swimming underwater. Rigel had a harder time of it. Ben found himself lagging behind, until he hooked two fingers through the high-tech collar and began to pull the dog along as he swam.

They turned right twice, until he could see the door at the end. It was thirty metres away. Ben felt cold as he realised there was almost no air left in this corridor. They'd have to swim the whole way without breathing, although Rigel could just about keep his nose above water. One of the men clearly had no problem with this. He swept ahead with a powerful breaststroke. The second man was struggling. Ben stuck with him. Two-thirds of the way along, he turned to Ben, eyes imploring. Ben didn't hesitate. He stuck the octopus mouthpiece over the man's mouth. The man's eyes rolled back in relief as oxygen filled his lungs.

The corridor lurched, tilted again. The ceiling was touching his head. Adrenaline flowed through Ben as the survival urge gripped him. Fingers still threaded through Rigel's collar, he surged for the open door. The platform was going down. This was the last chance they'd have.

Ben and Rigel emerged to a riot of sound – the blast of water cannons, the rumble of the fire. Swathes of steam and oily smoke billowed across the waves. And behind it all, he heard the throb of helicopter blades.

Scorpio was hovering close by. Julia had already dropped the ladder. The oil man who'd pushed ahead was the first to reach it. Seconds later, Ben was climbing it too, heaving Rigel up with him. The second survivor was a minute behind.

For a few moments, Ben just sat with Rigel, exhausted from the swim and the climb. The two survivors were the same. Too tired to talk, they just hugged each other.

Slowly, Ben began to focus on Julia's voice in his earpiece radio. It had started to function again properly once he'd escaped the sinking platform. He tried to catch a glimpse of Horizon Alpha as *Scorpio* turned in the air. The oil rig's accommodation block was almost gone now. Its ballast tanks and positioning rotors – which should have been deep underwater – were visible as the helicopter flew overhead.

Julia's voice was clearly audible over the intercom. 'This is *Scorpio*. Two Horizon Alpha survivors incoming, *Atlanta*. Permission to land.'

One of the oil workers was leaning back on his hands, staring at Ben. He looked amazed.

'You're just a kid.'

Ben handed the dripping gun to the man. 'What's a gun doing on an oil rig?'

'Terrorists,' replied the oil man. 'Ever since those oil company guys in Algeria got taken hostage and slaughtered, we got all sorts of anti-terrorist protocols. Pity they didn't work this time.'

'Terrorists did this?' Absent-mindedly, Ben began to stroke Rigel. The dog was exhausted by the swim. He'd laid his head across his front paws, ears flat and eyes closed.

The man gave a grim nod. 'Yesterday we had a visit from a platform supply vessel, *PSV-Macondo*. I heard one of them talking on his phone. In Arabic,' he added, with widened eyes.

'Speaking Arabic doesn't make you a terrorist,' Ben said, uncomfortably.

Ben's tone didn't seem to impress the oil man. 'The others called him something like Camzeen. That sounds Middle Eastern to me.'

'This fool is all about the conspiracy theories,' interrupted the second survivor. 'Take no notice. There was a systems failure. The BOP must have failed.'

'It did. And your power blew out,' Ben told them.

The second man nodded confidently. 'That's what I thought. We lost all but emergency communications. That's why we lost position over the well. The riser must be in a mess.'

'It is – it's all twisted up underneath.'

'You are all talking like this was an accident,' said the first man, his nostrils flaring. 'Meanwhile, whoever planted the bombs is getting away.'

'Bombs?' Ben repeated.

'Yeah, bombs. Something caused the BOP to fail. Gas builds up on the rig. Then – real conveniently – another explosion! You telling me that's a coincidence? No way. I'm telling you, that Camzeen guy – he knows something about it.'

They were landing now, on the spacious deck of *PSV-Atlanta*. It looked to be the size of a football pitch. Ben had never seen such a vessel before. The ship was around a hundred metres long with a wide open deck, easily large enough to land two helicopters simultaneously. A coastguard helicopter was already in the middle of the deck. It was taking on passengers, getting ready to leave.

When *Scorpio* touched down, Ben saw eyes on deck turn to gaze curiously at the distinctive aircraft.

Hey, Jason – I'd like to see you maintain secrecy after this, Ben thought.

The two survivors were out of *Scorpio* by the time Julia had found her way to the passenger cabin. Her stare was all icy disdain and barely contained fury.

'I know, I know,' Ben said, before she could get a word in.

The pilot really looked as though she might be about to slap him. 'If you were my kid, this would be major trouble for you.'

He decided to tough it out. 'But that's just it. I'm no one's. Not any more. And those two guys needed someone. They needed *me*.'

Julia seemed reluctant to let it go, but Ben could sense that she was under pressure of time. She checked the large timepiece on her left wrist. 'Truby wants you back, asap. You and the dog. He sent *Aquarius* for you. It's the only craft we could spare.'

'*Scorpio* is staying?'

'The oil won't stop coming up.' She gestured towards the pillar of black smoke about two hundred metres away. 'We're gonna help with the fire.'

Ben waited. It felt as though Julia were trying to find a way to word a particularly choice insult – one that even she was reluctant to use, but felt she had to.

She took a deep breath. 'Benedict. You and Rigel – you did well.'

CRAB WITH BEEF

A third aircraft was parked on the deck of *PSV-Atlanta*. But no one noticed it.

The only sign of *Aquarius*'s presence was Addison Nicole Dyer. She appeared to be standing casually towards the aft of the deck, one elbow cocked at an angle, apparently leaning on nothing more substantial than a cushion of air. Like Julia, she wore the full Gemini Force uniform.

Aquarius. And it was camouflaged!

Ben watched the two women greet each other with a fist bump. He watched rescue workers and survivors from Horizon Alpha mill around. They barely gave Addison and Julia a second glance. The Gemini Force uniform, Ben realised, was subtle. It didn't look radically different from the clothes worn by the oil platform workers, apart from the lack of a high-visibility jacket.

'Hey, James Bond. What's going on?' Addison delivered the line without blinking. Ben didn't miss her sardonic tone. Another dig at his reckless deed. But he was ready to handle whatever barbs they threw his way.

It was beginning to make sense now, what had happened to his mother. Ben felt like he could almost understand. Not all deaths were meaningless.

With a hint of a grin, Julia said, 'The kid rescued two of those Horizon Alpha men.'

Addison just nodded. 'I've got orders to fly him back to base. Maybe there'll be a hero's welcome. Or maybe not.'

Ben watched Julia move in front of Addison, until she was shielding her from almost all lines of sight on the deck.

'Addison will open the door. You and Rigel, get inside,' Julia said quietly to Ben.

Before he could object, Ben saw the lights of a cockpit control panel appear as if in a slice of air to Addison's right.

Aquarius.

The two women moved aside slightly as Rigel and Ben pushed past. Then, as if he'd stepped through a portal, Ben was inside the aircraft. Addison followed him.

'How did nobody see that?' Ben asked, amazed.

Addison was already buckling herself in. 'People see what they expect to see. When they witness something that seems to defy explanation, ninety-nine out of a hundred people will ignore it.'

'And one person might report it,' he said.

Addison only shrugged. 'They might. Gemini Force might even become another modern myth. The kind of thing that no serious person actually believes in. The more immediate situation, Ben, is that we took a risk today. Because of you. Paul has already freed five survivors – got them out of a burning structure. Now, instead of helping him, I'm taking care of you.'

More than a bit resentful, Ben also fastened his own safety belt. Rigel crawled reluctantly into the pet carrier that had been brought along on the rear seats. Ben watched Addison make the final flight checks.

He said. 'I'm not being funny, but what's one tiny extra aeroplane going to do for this rescue effort?' He pointed to the black smoke that still belched in the distance. The entire sky now carried its stain. Within, a huge orange fireball throbbed, yet still the fire crews fought. 'They've got a massive problem. The oil is still coming up from the well. They can't stop the fire. It won't be long before that oil platform ends up at the bottom of the sea.'

'Truby's got a plan – he's sending *Leo* to fetch a specially adapted stack of heavy-duty valves from a shipping manufacturer in China. I could have helped. But instead, I get to pick up the daredevil who decided to ...'

Ben was trying hard to ignore her comments. If he took them seriously, they would only infuriate him. 'Maybe you could try to find out who did this. One of the guys I rescued reckoned some terrorists might have done it.'

'Yeah,' Addison muttered. She didn't sound convinced either. 'We heard those theories too. Seems these days there's no explosions anywhere without someone accuses al-Qaeda.'

'I know. It's crazy, isn't it?'

'Well, now – it is and it isn't.'

'Meaning what?'

She turned to him with a subtle smile. 'Just 'cause you're paranoid, doesn't mean they're not out to get you. Get ready for lift.'

There was a sudden roar of engines as *Aquarius*'s vertical take-off began. Through the windshield, Ben could see that a dozen or so of the people on the deck had turned around and were watching their ascent. Their expressions didn't look more than vaguely interested. Not the reaction he'd have expected. Surely the witnesses to their departure were experiencing intense noise, the heat of the engines, a sudden stiff breeze?

Wouldn't they wonder where it was all coming from?

He said as much to Addison. She dismissed it with a shrug. 'That's why I turned off "invisibility" before I started the engines.'

'So people would have seen the plane appear from nowhere.'

'You ever see a UFO, Ben?'

'Me? Never.'

'Really? Huh. Most people, when you ask that question, they say the same thing. Then, maybe a few minutes later, they qualify it. One time they saw … And then they'll tell you some weird stuff. At the end, though, and this, Ben, in my experience is without exception, they'll go, "Anyhow, I guess I must have imagined it" or something like that.'

'What about the ones who report it?' Ben asked.

'Well, those people, they are few and far between. The sky is a strange place. Unexplained things happening in it all the time.'

They were in the air now, rising high above *PSV-Atlanta*. Directly ahead, the air was almost entirely dark, what was left of a leaden-grey sky blotted out by inky smoke.

It did seem that their departure hadn't raised more than a couple of eyebrows. Ben guessed that most passengers on *PSV-Atlanta* had enough to be worrying about.

'One of the guys I rescued was something of a conspiracy theorist. He swore blind that he'd heard an Arabic-speaking terrorist on Horizon Alpha, a few days ago. He was adamant that the bloke must have planted bombs.'

'An Arabic speaker?' Addison seemed, for the first time since picking Ben up, to be surprised by something that he'd said.

'Yeah. "Camzeen" he said his name was. It was yesterday. The guy was visiting from a platform supply vessel.'

'From *Atlanta*?'

'No, a different one – *Macondo*.'

'*PSV-Macondo*,' she said. 'I wonder.'

Then she was radioing Gemini Force One, routing the call directly through her earpiece. Ben couldn't catch the other side of the conversation.

She closed the communication. The aircraft tilted. It began to turn.

'What's going on?'

'I'm playing a hunch.'

Ben looked at Addison curiously, waiting for more.

She grinned. 'We're going to find the *PSV-Macondo*, Ben. Once in a while, you get served a crab salad with a sliver of beef in it. When that happens, look out.'

Now he was thoroughly confused. 'What?'

'You know, when something doesn't quite fit? Like crab with beef? *PSV-Macondo* is staffed by Venezuelans. Arabic isn't too well used there. If the US military trained me to be vigilant about one thing, it's noticing when Arabic is used in all the wrong kinds of contexts.'

'You think maybe this Camzeen guy *is* al-Qaeda?'

'Doubtful – but something doesn't add up and I think it's worth checking out.'

Ben shivered as his damp clothes began to chill in the aircraft's air-conditioning.

If he hadn't mentioned the Horizon Alpha worker's comments, Addison would be flying him straight back to Gemini Force One where food, a hot shower and dry, warm clothes awaited him. Instead, they were headed for yet another platform supply vessel. Where, Ben was fairly convinced, they'd find that whoever they were looking for had already left. Chances were it was some Arabic-speaking oil-industry worker who'd just happened to emigrate to South America.

One day, Ben reflected, *I'll have to learn when to keep my mouth shut.*

⎯ MACONDO ⎯

PSV-Macondo had almost reached the shores of Venezuela when Gemini Force located it. Addison took *Aquarius* high and flew at top speed, just under Mach 1. By the time they reached the platform supply vessel, it was ten nautical miles off the coast of Aruba, a small Caribbean island close to Venezuela.

Tropical Storm Isidore hadn't yet finished with the Caribbean. Towards the Cayman Islands, it was whipping up waves as high as twenty metres. The coast of Venezuela was getting the tail end of the cyclone. It made for a bumpy flight. Ben was dreading touch-down on the ship. It was slopping around in the waves, each lurch dropping the vessel by at least a metre.

The deck of *Macondo* was entirely deserted. At around fifty metres in length, the platform supply vessel was about half the size of *Atlanta*. The emptiness made it seem dauntingly large. It wasn't easy to land, with the deck pitching up and down. Eventually, Addison managed the landing, remaining in camouflage mode. For several minutes, Ben helped Addison to examine every on-board display that showed their surroundings.

She said, 'I got a bad feeling about this.'

'Got a gun?' Ben asked.

'No weapons,' she replied. 'Truby. He's a pacifist. Doesn't believe in them.'

'Fair play to him. But – until someone invents a force field that can block bullets, aren't we a bit vulnerable without them?'

Addison didn't answer that. Maybe she agreed with him, maybe not. Ben made a mental note to ask her, one day, about her reasons for quitting the US Air Force. She'd fought in Afghanistan. Perhaps she'd seen something really terrible.

'Ready to go?' Ben asked.

She finished typing something into a keyboard on the control panel. 'I'm sending Gemini Force One our coordinates. Out in the open sea, our GPS tracker doesn't always work.'

Cautiously, they exited *Aquarius*, taking Rigel with them. Then, one at a time, they made a beeline for the port side of the deck. The deck was flooded with a couple of centimetres of water. Making unsteady progress, they gripped the edge of the deck and headed for the bridge. It was just possible that all the crew were inside. Perhaps *Aquarius*'s arrival in camo mode had allowed them to land on the deck without creating a stir.

Once they'd found the bridge deck equally deserted, however, this possibility swiftly vanished. Still in radio contact, they split up – Addison going one way, Ben and Rigel another. Separately, they methodically searched the wheelhouse, then the upper and lower forecastle decks.

As he searched each silent corridor and empty room in turn, Ben became aware of an insidious sensation in the pit of his stomach. At first he thought maybe it was some kind of seasickness, or even a flashback to the panic-soaked moments when he'd been searching the flooded corridors of Horizon Alpha. Then, he'd felt as though something of the crew's terror had remained on board after they'd evacuated. It was the same here.

The echo of his footsteps in that cavernous sea vessel left an imprint on his mind. An unsettling feeling of solitude. The cold terror of *nothing*. He glanced down at his hands to see that all the hairs were standing to attention.

Only Rigel's presence and the occasional whisper of Addison's voice in his earpiece radio made him feel a little calmer.

Death had brushed close to Ben of late. It was as though he'd learned something of its smell and it was here on *Macondo*. Ben could practically taste it.

Nervously, he made his way to the tween deck, where the accommodation was housed. Addison was waiting, her back pressed against the corridor next to the nearest door. She motioned for him to be silent. Ben watched her push open the door in one swift move. From inside – silence. She poked her head around the door. 'You found nothing?'

Ben shook his head.

Addison sighed. 'Holy cow, we got the *Mary Celeste,* here.'

'What's *Mary Celeste*?'

'You never hear of it? The ghost ship. Famous case of a ship found drifting. Totally empty. Whole crew disappeared, leaving all their kit behind. Take a look inside this cabin.'

Ben felt a creeping sensation at the back of his neck as he peered into the cabin. Both bunks were made up, pillows plumped and carefully positioned at the heads of the beds. At the foot of each bed, there was a pile of neatly folded laundry: white underwear and black socks. On the single desk, there was a stack of three books and, lying casually next to these, was an iPad.

'They left in a hurry,' Ben remarked.

Addison regarded him with a critical eye. 'I think maybe it's time I got you off this ship.'

'What? We haven't finished searching yet. There's all the space under the main storage deck.'

'Something bad happened here, kid. It's time to leave. You said it yourself; we're not equipped to go looking for trouble.' Without waiting for his reply, Addison turned towards the staircase, heading up.

Then he heard it. A very faint moaning, barely audible. The sound of someone sick or in pain.

Ben's eyes met Addison's. She'd heard it too. Rigel's ears pricked up. He glanced at Ben, waiting for instructions. In a stern, commanding voice Ben said, 'Rigel, find, find, find!'

The dog rushed off down the corridor with Ben and Addison behind.

The sound had stopped.

Someone had heard them.

Rigel disappeared through the final door on the corridor of the tween deck. Addison and Ben heard a short, high bark.

Addison raised her eyebrows, questioning. Ben mouthed in reply, 'People.'

A second later they heard a pain-filled groan followed by an urgent cry. 'Move! He's got a gun!'

There was barely time for Ben and Addison to exchange a glance when from inside the cabin, a shot rang out. The sound was deafeningly loud inside that enclosed space. Ben heard the bullet ricochet along the corridor, no more than two metres ahead of where he stood.

'That's to show I mean business.' The voice was male, a lazy, confident drawl. No Arabic accent to speak of — in fact, Ben was fairly certain the speaker was British. 'Now, come out, with your hands in the air.'

Ben and Addison remained absolutely still.

After a brief pause, the voice said, 'Come on. I've got your bloody dog, for God's sake. You can't blame me for being cautious, can you? Presumably you've seen the rest of the ship by now?'

A muffled voice tried to speak. There was barely time to hear a snatched cry for help. Then silence.

Fear threatened to paralyse Ben. He was shocked by the intensity of it. There was a quality to this fear that he'd never encountered before on mountains or even in Horizon Alpha.

It felt like being hunted.

Inside that cabin, someone was toying with them. They'd managed to silence one person and Rigel too. The same *someone* might have got rid of everyone else in the crew.

Ben and Addison had been lured, rather effectively, to a place from which escape would be difficult.

Addison held Ben's gaze. She pointed a single finger towards the exit and mouthed, 'Run.'

LATITUDE, LONGITUDE

The next bullet whizzed past his left ear. Addison was already halfway down the corridor but Ben hadn't budged. Rigel was trapped with that maniac. Ben wasn't going to abandon him!

'Stop!' came the British voice.

Addison must have realised that Ben wasn't following her because she stopped almost immediately. Her feet skidded across the metallic floor as the ship pitched hard and abruptly to their left.

Rigel let out an agonised squeal.

'I'm a good shot,' came the voice again, 'but it's dark in here, the boat is tipping all over the place and I'm out of practice.' Then, furiously, the man shouted, 'If you want to risk the dog's life, or your own, take another step. Go ahead.'

Ben looked at Addison, shook his head and mouthed, 'Don't.'

'Good decision. Hands where I can see them. Now come down here.'

They did as he said. The man had moved partially into the corridor now and Ben peered closely at him. He stood propped in the doorframe, which seemed a pretty efficient way to maintain some stability in the stormy conditions. He was well over six feet tall, with short, wavy hair and thick, prominent eyebrows, almost black in colour. His skin was sallow, almost olive-coloured. Dressed in black jeans and a midnight-blue, military-style bomber jacket, he could have passed as South American or Mediterranean. But from his accent Ben was certain that the man had been born or at least grown up in Britain. It wasn't a public-school accent, so he probably wasn't a foreigner who'd gone to a boarding school in the UK. It sounded vaguely northern, if anything.

When he saw how Ben scrutinised him, the man let out a guffaw. 'Think you're going to live to identify me? Well, we'll see about that.'

Ben risked a quick glance at Rigel through the open door. The dog was on the threshold of the room, licking a wound in his front paw. Every now and again he lapped at the floor where blood had spattered. His low, incessant whines tugged at Ben's heart.

'All right. Now I want you to take that mutt and lock him in the storage locker. You'll find one on the corridor, a little further up. Get him inside and close the door properly. I want to hear a good slam. Then turn around and get back over here. Keep your hands where I can see them the whole time. Remember there's a Glock pointed at you and no shortage of bullets.'

Ben waited for a signal from Addison. After a couple of seconds, reluctantly, she gave the nod. They followed his instructions about Rigel. Ben planted a kiss on the dog's head before gently putting him into the locker. Addison closed the door with a heavy *clunk*.

They made their way back cautiously. Each time the ship rocked, Ben felt certain that he might be thrown forward, down the corridor and into a shower of bullets.

Ben felt his breath freeze. He released it a second or so later. It came out in broken, terrified chunks. The man with the gun grabbed hold of a handful of Ben's jacket. Ben forced himself not to recoil or struggle. He felt himself pushed down to his knees. Then, without a pause, the man whipped his pistol against Ben's ear.

Pain exploded in Ben's head. He fell forward onto his hands, feeling a warm trickle of blood run down his neck from his ear. The ringing in his head went on for a long time and he vaguely heard himself moan. Eventually, the agitated sound of Addison's voice began to filter through to him.

'... just a kid! We're not the police. We're not looking for trouble.'

'Not police, no, I guessed that.' With the muzzle of his weapon, he poked Addison's uniform badge. 'Gemini Force? What's that?'

Addison hesitated. 'We're rescue workers.'

'Do-gooders? Should have done *yourselves* some good and stayed out of things that don't concern you.'

'Where are the crew of *Macondo*?'

'Sea burial,' came the terse reply. 'Best thing for a sailor, wouldn't you agree?'

In a daze, Ben stared at the floor. He could taste blood in his mouth.

'Two of you. Huh.' The man reached back into the room inside which, Ben presumed, his latest victim was now dead. A second later, he pushed a wooden chair in front of Ben and tossed Addison a spool of nylon rope. A sadistic note entered the man's voice. 'Tie the boy to the chair. Or I'll shoot him right in his pretty face.'

He leaned back against the door. 'You're going to tell me everything there is to tell about Gemini Force. If you choose to refuse then I'm going to have some fun with you. Maybe it'll be waterboard time. That's how you people like to deal with your enemies, isn't it?'

Ben spat blood. '"You people"?'

The sardonic comment earned him a swift kick to the ribs. Pain began to sweep through his chest – a deep, cold ache that seemed to alternate with burning.

Addison was apparently oblivious to Ben's suffering. In a hard, professional voice she demanded, 'Who are you?'

The man let out an exasperated sigh. 'Grasp the situation, girly. *I'm* asking the questions. Now, boy, straighten up and face me.'

Ben forced himself to comply. He was rewarded with a hard, open-palmed slap to the right side of his face. He shook his head slightly, trying to recover from the blow.

The man bent forward. He glared at Ben. Nervously, Ben eyed the Glock. Its blunt muzzle was still aimed at him.

'You both need to understand something.' The man lowered his voice to a chilling whisper. 'There is a chance you'll get out of this. A *small* chance, admittedly, but play nice and it could happen.'

With the gun still on Ben, the man turned to Addison. 'Now, talk. What's Gemini Force? Don't bother to lie. I'm good at telling truth from lies.'

Addison said, 'What've you heard about us?'

The man's face grew thunderously dark. There was a ruthless edge to his voice. 'Final warning. Tie the boy up and answer the damn question. Or we'll start the death of a thousand cuts. The first bullet goes in the kid's left knee, the second one goes in the right. Then I start shooting bits off him.'

Ben sat in the chair and Addison began, slowly, to tie Ben to it. She spoke slowly, too. 'We're a rescue agency. We ... we go where we're needed. We've got a few rescue vehicles. We ...'

The man waved the pistol, irritated. 'Get specific. Where's your base? Who's in charge? How many vehicles? Describe them.'

'We got some ... four rescue vehicles.'

'Where. Is. Your. Base?'

Again, Addison hesitated. When she spoke, Ben heard a note of desperation enter her voice.

'It's in the Caribbean.'

'I guessed that much, *moron*. Latitude, longitude?'

A powerful wave lifted and then dropped the ship. The room lurched violently to the right. As it did, Ben heard a dull, slithering sound. In the next instant, a male body slid from beneath the lower bunk inside the cabin and came to rest in the doorway. The throat had been slashed from ear to ear. The eyes were wide open, frozen in horror. Blood had soaked the navy-blue V-necked sweater of the victim's uniform and left a long trail of blood from under the bunk.

A cruel smile touched the lips of their captor.

'Hey, look who decided to drop in to give you a quick word of advice. Better listen to this bloke or you'll end up just the same way.' With his free hand, the man reached into the inside pocket of his jacket. When his hand emerged, it was brandishing a blood-stained hunting knife.

⬛ TERRORIST ⬛

The scent of Ben's blood must have reached Rigel, because he began to bark. It wasn't a bark that Ben recognised – it certainly wasn't one of Rigel's trained patterns of alert. After a moment, Ben realised it was the raw, uncontrolled pattern of an animal in distress.

Rigel had gone happily into the locker – that was how much he trusted Ben. Now his anxiety was over-riding that trust. The sound of his claws scraping against the inside of the door echoed down the corridor.

Their captor listened. 'Pooch misses you. It's lucky for him that I like dogs or I'd give him a sea burial, too.'

Ben stared, defiant. 'They're going to find you, you know. ANPECO know you're working for al-Qaeda.'

For a second, a smile of genuine amusement crossed their captor's lips. 'ANPECO know, do they?'

In a warning voice, Addison told Ben, 'Be quiet.'

'No, no,' the man said, taunting. 'Tell me more!'

Biting his lip, Ben tried to shift around so that he could see Addison. When the man swung for him this time, Ben swerved. The chair tipped over. He fell back-wards.

Then they heard it. Rigel's barking was suddenly louder – and getting closer by the second.

Somehow, he'd got out of the locker.

In the next moment a ball of furious energy came hurtling up the corridor. Rigel dived at Ben on the floor, beside himself with joy and relief.

For a second or two, their captor was totally thrown. He just stood, gun in one hand, knife in the other. 'Stay where you are!'

Once he'd realised that Rigel wasn't threatening him, he seemed to calm down.

'You.' He gestured to Addison. 'Finish tying the boy up. Then we're going to put the dog somewhere safe.' He paused. 'Good job the creature didn't go for me, or he'd be dead.'

'He's not an attack dog,' Ben blurted. 'He's trained to find injured people. He smelled my blood.'

A moment later, the chair had been righted and Ben's wrists were securely bound to the back of it. The man tested each knot, then stepped past him.

'Bring the dog. Let's go,' he told Addison.

A couple of seconds passed. Then, without warning, from behind Ben's head a hand clapped around his mouth. In his ear he heard the hissed words, 'It's Julia. Stay in the chair.'

In the next minute Ben felt his bindings go slack.

In a distant corridor, a door slammed shut. He heard the sound of footsteps returning. Wide-eyed, Ben turned to face Julia. She signalled for silence, pulled herself back into the shadows against the wall.

'Wait for my signal. Go for his legs,' she whispered to Ben.

'He's got a gun …'

Julia merely nodded. Ben turned his attention to the ropes. If their captor looked, he'd see that the restraints were now loose. Addison approached, her hands raised level with her head. Ben began to turn the chair, as if to make space for them to come past, but also to hide his hands and the slackened ropes.

As the man and Addison reached Ben, Addison stumbled slightly and Julia's voice erupted.

'Now!'

There wasn't time to think of a better move. Ben simply swung a brutal kick at the man's legs.

Everything happened fast. A crack of gunfire. It was right next to Ben's head. A sudden, agonised cry. Julia on the floor. Blood pooling beneath her. Addison, whirling to face their attacker.

Ben dropped the ropes and shot to his feet. He pulled back a fist. His first blow connected with the back of the man's head.

The man faltered. He began to turn. The gun was in his hand.

But Addison was alert now. She kicked high and hard. The weapon went flying. For a millisecond they all watched as it arced through the air, over the bunks in the cabin on their right, and clattered against the wall, rattling its way to the floor.

Then Ben lunged at the man's left hand. Addison

shoulder-barged their captor's right flank. And, with two assailants, he was knocked off balance.

A pulse of adrenaline hit Ben's brain. He felt a surge of blood-rage. Viciousness like he'd never known was pumping into him. He and Addison shoved the man heavily against the wall. They pushed their full weights against him, pinning both legs.

Through clenched teeth, Addison said, 'Who are you?'

The man's knife hand was immobilised but still he gripped the blade. Ben gasped with the effort of trying to prise his fingers apart. The man was ludicrously strong. In another minute he would overpower them both.

Behind them, Julia groaned. Ben tilted his head enough to catch a glimpse. She'd flipped over and lay sprawled on the floor. A dark patch soaked the left side of her abdomen. Underneath, blood oozed, like an oil slick.

Somewhere Ben could hear Rigel going crazy. The racket of the dog's incessant barking coupled with a rusty stench of blood mixed with fear. As Ben grappled with their captor, he could feel his concentration slipping.

Julia was reaching underneath the bed. She pulled out the gun. Holding it in both hands, she yelled, 'Get back so I can shoot!'

Ben felt the man relax under his grip. He heard him say, 'All right, OK.' Then the knife was in Ben's hand. He stepped back. Addison did the same.

'So you're not going to shoot?' the man said, with a relieved smile.

Julia winced. 'You bet I am, if you move a muscle.'

'Son of a—'Addison punched the man hard in the belly. He grunted but, a moment later, he laughed in her face.

'Honey, don't,' Julia warned Addison. She propped herself up on one arm, rose to a sitting position. Ben could hear the agony in her every movement.

Addison took the gun. She pressed it firmly and deliberately against the man's temple.

'Tell me your name or *so help me* I will blow your brains all over this cabin.'

'Khamsin,' he breathed, eventually. 'But you already knew that.' Softly, he chuckled, 'Al-Qaeda!'

'We're supposed to believe you're not?' Addison demanded.

'You can think what you bloody well like.'

Julia's voice broke in. '*Aquarius*, you gotta get me out of here. I'm losing blood pretty fast.'

Khamsin said, smugly, 'Yes, *Aquarius,* better take care of your friend. She's not looking too good.' He turned to Ben. 'English, American and the other woman – what is she? Portuguese? Israeli? Brazilian? Quite an international crew, you Gemini Force lot. Who's in charge?'

Abruptly, he spun around. Khamsin fled.

GROUND-POUNDER

Ben began to give chase but Addison grabbed his elbow. 'Leave it. We're not cops.'

'He's the one who planted the bombs!'

'You sure changed your tune.'

'I'm not sure I believe that line about him not being al-Qaeda. Just because he's white? There are white *jihadis* these days.'

Addison looked doubtful. 'He seemed pretty amused by the idea.'

'Maybe. I guess we'll see,' Ben said. 'We'd better get Julia to the deck.'

They freed Rigel and then, between the two of them, gently raised Julia to her feet. She could walk only with difficulty. Rigel padded alongside them, subdued. It took them several long, painful minutes to walk Julia through the corridor, up the staircase and onto the upper deck. The storm continued to toss the ship on huge waves. Once they were out in the open, they had to fight against persistent spray and the violent motions of the vessel.

Scorpio was parked in the middle of the main deck. It couldn't have been more than five metres from the still-cloaked *Aquarius*. Rigel leaped aboard the moment the passenger cabin door was opened. With the utmost care, they eased Julia into the cabin after him and strapped her into a reclined seat.

Ben followed Addison into the cockpit of *Scorpio*. He looked around, wiped a blood-smeared hand on his jeans. 'How is Khamsin going to get away?'

'My guess? He's hiding,' Addison said. 'Waiting for us to leave. Watching.'

'What are we going to do with *Aquarius*? We don't want to leave it here for Khamsin to find!'

'You're telling me,' Addison muttered. 'Ben, you think you can fly *Scorpio*?'

In disbelief, he said, 'Are you joking?'

'We have to get Julia to the nearest hospital and I mean the very nearest. That means the island of Aruba. Ben, I'm not asking you to take off or land. I'll take us into the air. Then I'll hand the controls over to you. All you need to do is hold us steady and follow the course I set. I'll be right here. When we reach the coast, I'll take over and put us down somewhere.'

'You just want me to hold the cyclic?' Ben's hand hovered over the helicopter's main directional control.

She had already turned away, preoccupied. 'Yes, and use the torque pedals to help keep us level.'

'What are *you* going to be doing?'

When Addison turned back she was holding something in her hand. It looked like the joystick controls to a computer game.

'I'm going to be flying *Aquarius* – by remote.'

'No, really?'

'It's a safety feature. Truby insisted on adding it to all the GF aircraft. They can all be flown by remote, with one pretty big proviso – the pilot needs a line of sight to the vehicle.'

Ben stared back at the deck of *Macondo*. 'And we have a line of sight.'

'You got it. Now, we've failed to secure *Macondo*. Khamsin may have headed for the bridge. By the time we get back from Aruba, he could have sailed this ship fifty nautical miles in any direction. Remote is our only way of getting *Aquarius* back.' Addison placed a hand on his upper arm. 'Ben, you've been pretty hardcore today. Maybe you're a ground-pounder at heart, but I need you to do this.'

'Hell, yeah, I'm on board!' he cried. Ben closed a fist around the cyclic. He touched a foot to one of the torque pedals. *Time to focus.*

Gently, Addison eased his hand off the control. 'Good to see you're keen. Just let me get her into the air first.'

Addison took control. The rotor blades began to turn. Ben felt the landing skids lift away from the deck. Addison took *Scorpio* into the air until it hovered directly above the deck. 'OK,' she said, nodding. 'I'm going to talk you through this, Ben. Concentrate and do exactly what I tell you.'

He licked his dry, cracking lips. 'Will do.'

'Right. Take the cyclic. Keep a light, but really light,

touch on the torque. Really, you're gonna do most of this with the cyclic. You're gonna be gentle.'

Ben took a breath and wrapped his fingers around the control. He sensed the weight and power of the helicopter transmitted, through the cyclic, to his hand.

I'm flying a helicopter.

Addison took a few moments to explain what he needed to do and convince herself that he was doing everything right, then turned her attention to the remote control for *Aquarius*. Through the lower corner of the cockpit window, Ben could see the apparently empty space on deck that he knew was occupied by the camouflaged aircraft.

A drop of salty sweat touched his lips. He wiped it away with a sleeve.

Addison touched a button on the panel. Ben both felt and heard the throaty firing of the aeroplane's engines. Still, nothing was visible.

'OK. We're almost ready to go. You're going to move us over towards the starboard side of the ship. Then I'll bring *Aquarius* up. Ben, I want you to keep checking your nine o'clock, keep *Aquarius* at the same distance at all times. All the way to the coast. Gently, Ben.'

Addison touched another control and in the air beside them, about fifty metres away, the camouflage dissipated. An aircraft appeared to materialise from nothing. It began to fly forwards.

'OK, Ben. Match speed. Keep *Aquarius* on your nine.'

The wounds on his ribs and head throbbed, a steady

pulse of pain. The tension was beginning to get to him. One of Gemini Force's aircraft was at his mercy. One wrong move and he might fly it and himself, Rigel, Addison and Julia into *Aquarius* and a blazing ruin.

But it was either this or risk losing *Scorpio* or *Aquarius* to Khamsin. And not just the aircraft, but also whatever secret information the on-board systems had stored about Gemini Force One.

A memory of his mother's death, only two days ago, flashed into Ben's mind. But he knew this wasn't the time. He had to focus now. The speed at which he was able to close the thought down came as quite a shock. And, with it, came a little more understanding of Jason Truby.

— SHEAR FORCE —

They flew in tandem: Ben stiff with concentration, steering *Scorpio*, Addison's attention split between the occasional check on Ben and a more vigilant eye on the empty aircraft that flew less than fifty metres to their immediate left. When Ben found himself listening out for the sound of Rigel's low whining from *Scorpio*'s passenger cabin, he had to stop himself. This was no time to think about anything except the task at hand.

Ten exhilarating yet exhausting minutes later, Ben handed the cyclic back to Addison. She had landed *Aquarius* on a wide, isolated beach on the south-west coast of Aruba, while *Scorpio* hovered above. Ben was still high on the buzz as he watched Addison activate *Aquarius*'s camouflage.

'Julia, how are you doing?' Ben asked, speaking through the intercom into the passenger cabin.

'You'd better get me to a hospital fast,' came a tired, yet steady, reply. 'I think that jerk pretty much gave me an appendectomy by bullet.'

'How about Rigel?'

There was a definite warmth to her reply. 'Oh, he's right here beside me. Two wounded soldiers comforting each other. Seriously, though, let's get going.'

Relieved at Julia's tone and her words, Ben watched *Aquarius* disappear among the palm trees and drying seaweed. *Scorpio* rose higher, into a darkening sky.

They landed in the car park of the island's only hospital minutes later. Addison sent Ben into the hospital to get help, which returned in the form of two orderlies and a hospital gurney. Ben stayed with Julia all the way to the operating theatre, holding the Brazilian woman's hand as she grew paler with every painful jolt of the gurney.

Ten hours later, they arrived back at Gemini Force One. Truby, Paul, Lola and Nina were waiting to greet them when they landed in the Gemini Force Three hangar pod. Both the medics were dressed in scrubs. Paul and Lola disappeared into the passenger cabin with a stretcher. They emerged carrying Julia between them and deposited her gently onto a waiting gurney. Nina stepped up alongside, beginning to examine the patient as Julia was whisked away to the waiting lift that would take her from the depths of the lowered hangar pod to the main decks of the base. Julia's wound had turned out to be pretty serious. She'd had to lose a short section of her gut, including her appendix. Thankfully, the hospital in Aruba had a surgeon with a great deal of experience in gunshot wounds.

When the local police had shown interest, Truby had pulled strings to get Julia out of there fast. He had bought them ten precious minutes during which no one was quite sure who was in charge – the police, the hospital administrator or the surgeon.

Those ten minutes had been enough to get Julia and her intravenous drip back aboard Scorpio.

Ben had been hoping to use the flight back to base to plan what he'd say to Truby, but exhaustion had got the better of him and, within five minutes of taking off, he'd been asleep.

Now, as Ben disembarked with Rigel in his arms, he risked a quick glance in Truby's direction. There had to be some almighty rollicking coming his way any time now. As Rigel licked his ear, Ben found himself wishing that Truby would get on with it.

But Truby, it seemed, had other things on his mind. He spoke quietly to Addison at enough distance that Ben couldn't catch all they were saying. She seemed to be updating him on what had happened aboard *Macondo*. They started to stroll towards the lift just as it deposited Lola, Paul, Nina and Julia at the main deck, above. By the time Ben and Rigel had joined Truby and Addison, the lift was back down on the hangar-pod floor.

And still, Truby gave Ben the silent treatment.

Once back on the main deck, Addison removed her helmet, peeled off her jacket and hung it in one of the lockers around the circular sitting room. She grabbed a snack bar from a box in the kitchenette area and sank into a chair. Ben watched her do all this before daring to turn to Truby, who hadn't moved.

'Go on. Let me have it,' Ben sighed.

Truby hesitated. 'Is that your apology?'

Stubbornly, Ben shook his head. 'I'm not going to apologise.'

To Ben's surprise, Truby said, 'Ben, let's stick a pin in this because, right now, Gemini Force and ANPECO are about to make history.'

His interest suddenly deflected, Ben responded, 'Oh, how?'

Truby just smiled and, leaving Ben with Rigel, headed over to the command centre.

The area was in near-darkness except for the light from the various high-definition display screens. Ben approached, a little hesitant. He watched for a few minutes, listening to Dietz and Truby talking to James and Tim over the radio.

On one screen was an underwater image of what looked like a metallic claw wrapped around a narrow tube.

Dietz said, 'Tim, can you move your camera in closer? They're going to try to shear again.'

Noticing Ben close by, Truby turned to him. 'What you're looking at is the oil platform's riser with a giant, remote-controlled shear about to tear it right across. It's a tough job – those claws have to get through a half-metre pipe that has a massively thick wall. *Pisces* has dropped a remote camera down to the bottom of the sea to monitor the shear.'

Dietz seemed to only now become aware of Ben

– and Addison, who had also wandered over. If he had any harsh thoughts towards Ben, he didn't show them.

'They've tried to shear through the riser six times already. It just won't give,' he remarked.

'They're going to cut through the riser … and then presumably they're going to cap the well?' Ben asked. An intelligent question might at least distract from his act of basic recklessness.

He was relieved to note Truby's apparent approval of the comment as Truby replied, 'That's the historic part. No one's ever capped a well this deep.'

Ben said, 'Do they know that the shear is powerful enough?'

'They tested it onshore but it's slippery down there,' Truby explained.

Tim's voice came over the radio. 'Tell ANPECO to rotate the shear by three degrees. Looks to me like it's getting caught on one of the earlier attempts.'

There was a pause while Gemini Force One relayed the message. Then Dietz said, 'OK. Eighth try.' He turned to Ben.

'What's Gemini Force's role, then?' Ben asked.

Dietz replied, 'Toru flew the valve stack in from Aquamachine in China. They're lowering it into the ocean as we speak. It should get down to the riser in the next fifteen minutes but, unless they can shear through the riser, it'll all be for nothing.'

'It's no good,' said Truby, without turning around. 'That shear just isn't doing it.'

Over the radio, James Winch's voice said, tersely, 'Tell them to try again.'

'Nine times? Surely if it hasn't worked by now ...?' Dietz murmured.

There was a tense pause. All eyes were on the screens that showed the riser in the jaws of the giant shear, as well as the progress of the stack towards the bottom of the ocean.

'All right. They're going for it one more time,' James reported.

When it happened, even Ben saw it. A faint trickle of darker fluid began to spool upwards from the riser.

Dietz cried out, 'Oil!'

Truby said, 'It's working! It's getting through!'

Over the various radio channels, Ben heard the cheers of ANPECO staff. On the display he could see an increasing volume of oil escape the riser, until the view from Tim's remote underwater camera was completely obscured by it.

He turned to Truby. 'What happens now?'

Truby clapped a hand to Ben's shoulder. 'Now we have to get the stack of valves into position over the open riser. Then we try to close them. Each valve we close makes the job a little bit easier. If we can close all four, then we're in business. The oil well is capped, the spillage stops. And ANPECO can begin the job of cleaning up the sea.'

'Sounds *immense*.' Ben began to smile.

Jason Truby didn't return the smile. 'Indeed it is. You, on the other hand, Ben, have a lot of explaining to do.'

➤ EMMA ➤

When Truby finally reacted to Ben's rogue rescue, it wasn't how Ben had expected.

Once Nina Atalas was satisfied that the surgeon on Aruba had made a good enough job of Julia's emergency surgery, Ben had taken his own turn in the medical room. With Julia sleeping off the effects of the anaesthetic in one curtained corner of the room, it had been Lola who'd patched up a slightly battered Ben.

Another hour later and Ben was still sitting in the command centre, waiting to be summoned to an audience with Truby. As he waited, Ben remembered how he'd watched his mother close the doors on a private meeting with Truby. When she'd emerged, she and Addison had been set on their path to joining Gemini Force.

Yet it had been Ben who'd pushed her final doubts away. Caroline Brandis-Carrington had joined Truby's rescue agency because of Ben. Because of that, she was dead.

These thoughts stirred with the searing, fresh memories of Ben's more recent exploits on Horizon Alpha and then *PSV-Macondo*. His ribs were bruised from Khamsin's attack; his left cheekbone had needed three stitches. Another centimetre up, Lola Reyes had told him, and he'd have lost the eye.

Four of the nine screens at the command centre were showing the successful capping of the oil well beneath Horizon Alpha. Tim and James were on their way back to Gemini Force One, inside *Pisces*. Toru was already on the base. Truby had opened four bottles of champagne and the crew were tipping the wine back as they watched.

The capped well wasn't their only triumph. So far, Truby had exerted enough persuasion with the senior staff at ANPECO to ensure that the few employees who'd been aware of Gemini Force's involvement would remain silent. Their secret was still safe – for now. It was as safe as a confidentiality agreement, anyhow. Ben's father hadn't rated such agreements too highly. 'A really juicy secret will always find its way out,' he used to say.

Ben wasn't surprised not to be invited to share the champagne. Being overlooked entirely, however, felt pretty rotten. He couldn't even talk to Jasmine. Michael Dietz had flown his daughter back to Cozumel Airport himself while Ben was battling Khamsin.

He got up to leave. On his way to the sitting room Ben reached down to pat Rigel, who was limping along beside him, one paw now neatly bandaged, courtesy of Lola.

'Feeling sorry for yourself?' Truby asked.

Ben looked up in surprise. Truby had strolled over from the command centre and now regarded Ben with an air of impatience. He didn't wait for a response to his question. 'Well, let's go.'

Ben hesitated.

Truby said, 'Time to go. Leave Rigel – he'll be fine on the base.'

'What? But I ... I need to say goodbye to Addi and Julia and the others,' Ben blurted.

'No goodbyes today,' Truby told him, with a hint of irritation. He turned and headed for the helo-deck. Clearly, he expected Ben to follow.

So that's how it was going to be. Truby wanted him off the base and he was going to be a dick about it. Disappointment weighed heavy on Ben's frame. But he stood firm.

'I can't leave without Rigel,' he called after Truby. 'Or without seeing the others.'

'Jeez, Ben,' Truby said, turning. 'Some army officer you're gonna make. You don't much like to follow orders, do you?'

Ben steeled himself. 'Not when the orders don't make sense.'

'Soldier, relax. You'll see your buddies again – you have my word. Now – do I gotta *make* you get into the chopper?'

Overcome with curiosity, Ben followed Truby into the Sikorsky.

The base began to rise out of the sea. It was dark outside, pitch black. Ben knew that Gemini Force One's location had been carefully selected for its shallow waters and safe distance from the shipping lanes. In better weather, they might have to worry about a random passing yacht or a fishing boat but, with Tropical Storm Isidore still raging off the coast of Colombia, the Caribbean would be unusually empty.

'Are you going to put the invisibility on?' Ben asked.

Truby gave just a hint of a friendly smile. 'I think tonight we'll get away without it.'

Moments later they were flying out of Gemini Force One. Truby had taken off with the most minimal light setting that Ben had seen so far. Apart from a few pale blue LEDs on the surface of the helo-deck, you would barely know that there was anything present in the inky black of the waves.

The tension of waiting for Truby to speak was almost unbearable and it was at least five more minutes before he said anything. Then, to Ben's surprise, he said gently, 'How're you holding up, kid?'

With a dry throat, Ben swallowed. 'Uh. Good. Still in shock, I think.'

'It won't really hit you for days.' A thoughtful pause. 'Especially if you keep trying to distract yourself by risking your own life.'

There was a lot that Ben wanted to say right then but he didn't dare to start. He couldn't quite judge how angry Truby might be.

The lights of Cozumel appeared on the horizon. Truby began to drop the helicopter. Ben watched the elevation fall on the display. The controls made a kind of sense to him now – he was no longer scared of them. For just a moment, he allowed himself to feel proud of that. That feeling gave him the courage to finally open his mouth.

'Give me another chance.'

Truby glanced at Ben. 'Another chance?'

'Yeah. I won't screw up so badly next time. I saved those two men, didn't I?'

'Yes. You did.'

Encouraged, Ben continued. 'I'll get better, I promise. I'll train. Get stronger. Be better at diving. I'll learn whatever you want me to learn. I'll train Rigel.'

'Rigel was a big help.'

'Yes. Yes! He was, wasn't he? Mum would have been so proud of him.'

'Ben, she would have been proud of *you.*'

In slow amazement, Ben gazed at Truby. 'You're not angry, then?'

'Angry? No. A little baffled as to what I'm going to do about you ... yeah. Definitely, that.'

'If you're not angry, then why are you making me leave GF One?'

'There is someone I want you to meet, but GF One isn't the place for it.'

The red-haired woman was waiting for them on the patio of Truby's villa. She'd been given a glass of iced tea and was sipping from it, watching water flow into a Japanese bamboo fountain and over the collection of smooth black-and-white pebbles at the base of the red ceramic bowl.

Truby greeted her like an old friend, with a kiss to each cheek. Ben guessed that she was about the same age as Truby, which he knew to be sixty. Although, in her lightweight black leather jacket, indigo jeans and wedge sandals, she dressed a good deal younger.

The woman held on to Truby's hands for a moment. She gazed into his eyes, fondly. Then she turned piercing blue eyes to Ben and pressed her painted orange-red lips together, considering.

'Good day, Benedict. You can call me Emma.'

Her accent was American, gentle and courteous. Ben shook the hand that Emma offered.

'Is that your real name?' he asked.

'No. I can't tell you my real name or what I do.'

Ben raised an eyebrow. 'Why not? Are you a spy?'

BLUE LIGHTS

Truby seemed mildly embarrassed by Ben's question. 'Better we let Emma ask the questions.'

Emma took an iPad Mini from her inside pocket. She showed the screen to Ben: twelve photo-portraits. All of them clean-shaven, dark-haired men in their thirties.

'These photos are the closest the face-match software could find to the description that you, Julia and Addison gave to Jason. Which one is Khamsin?'

Ben examined each image. 'None of them.'

She flicked onto the next screen. 'What about these?'

They kept going. Ben focused on each screen. After thirty or forty screens-worth, he began to tire. The features of all those men began to blur into each other.

Until the familiar leaped off the screen. Even seeing the man's face made Ben's pulse race.

'That's him.'

Emma touched the photo, enlarged it. An image of Khamsin filled the screen.

'Minos Winter,' she said, at length. 'You're sure?'

Ben blinked. 'It's him. His name isn't Khamsin?'

'A pseudonym, I should think. In Arabic it means "desert wind". And Minos Winter does indeed seem – thus far – to have been rather elusive.'

Truby said, 'Who is Minos Winter?'

'A British citizen,' Emma sighed. 'Not a criminal.'

'I beg to differ,' Ben said, pointing to the three neat stiches on his face.

'I mean, he's not known to be violent,' Emma explained. 'He's on a US database for minor offences, such as speeding and absconding to Britain without paying the tickets.' She peered at Ben. 'Are you absolutely certain? Because Mr Winter has a very powerful employer.'

'Who?'

'I'm not going to say his name but he is connected to the Saudi royal family.'

'The Saudi royals ... Wasn't Osama Bin Laden mates with them?' Ben asked.

'I can't comment ...' Emma said.

Ben continued, 'So Khamsin *is* in al-Qaeda?'

She shook her head. 'Unlikely. It may, however, be the impression that Mr Winter was intending to give.'

Truby tapped through some of the links on the iPad. 'His employer owns a very large oil company.'

Ben said, 'You think another oil company has it in for ANPECO? Why? Aren't those Middle Eastern oil companies way bigger than ANPECO?'

'They are now. But in the future, they may not be.' Truby handed the iPad to Ben. A newspaper article from a Western Australian newspaper was accompanied by the photo of an oil derrick in the middle of a Mars-red desert.

ANTILLEAN PETROLEUM CORPORATION A MAJOR INVESTOR IN GIANT KALBARRI OIL FIND

'It's from last year,' Truby said. 'Trillions of dollars' worth of shale oil, they reckon, under all that Australian rock and sand. And eighty per cent of it belongs to the people who own ANPECO.'

Ben was getting confused now. 'So I guess they're not all that bothered about losing Horizon Alpha?'

'I should think they're very bothered,' Emma said, a tad acidly. 'The money from Horizon Alpha oil was going to pay for the exploration of the Kalbarri field. Now the only way they'll ever exploit that Australian find is by bringing in new, outside investors.'

'And behind those investors,' Truby said, 'you can bet your bottom dollar you'll find the guy that Minos Winter works for. Whose company, if I'm not wrong, will become all but irrelevant if ANPECO puts that Australian oil field to work. Looks like Minos Winter has bought his employer some valuable time.'

'It's industrial espionage?'

'On a grand scale,' Emma confirmed. 'Mr Winter must be quite the resourceful fellow. This has the hallmarks of a covert military operation. I bet he's got an interesting background. It's going to be fun hunting around. I think, young Ben, that we owe you a vote of thanks. This guy's cover story looks pretty solid. I doubt we'd ever have happened across him – not with him keeping such a low profile.'

'I told you that Gemini Force would stir up the occasional hornet's nest,' Truby said to Emma.

'And you were right.' She smiled at him. 'I'm glad I fought for you.'

'It's thanks to Emma that we've got our privileged status with the US government,' Truby told Ben. 'I promised we'd share information when we could.'

'Are you CIA? NSA? DoD? The other one?' Ben asked with interest.

'The "other one"?'

'I can never remember all the secret agencies,' Ben sighed.

'If I were part of any of those, I wouldn't be able to say,' Emma told him.

'Oh my *word*. Do you actually *run* one of them? I bet you do.'

In spite of herself, Emma chuckled at Ben's urgent questions.

Truby, however, remained grave. 'Seriously, Ben, quit it.'

Emma took the iPad from Truby. 'Jason, I have to get going now. I've got a meeting at eight tomorrow morning.'

'No rest for the wicked,' he replied, without a trace of humour.

She looked for a last time at Ben. Chestnut-red fronds of her fringe drooped over her eyes, giving her, for a moment, a playful air. 'I hope we'll meet again, Benedict

Carrington. I met your father a few times. He was quite the host.'

Ben tried to smile. It could get pretty disconcerting, meeting strangers who claimed to have known his father. Sometimes it felt like the rest of the world had seen more of him than Ben had.

Then she was gone. Minutes later, Ben heard the sound of a helicopter taking off in the villa's back yard.

The main house was empty now as the domestic servants had gone to their own quarters. Truby went to the kitchen, opened the fridge, threw Ben a can of Diet Coke. He made two sandwiches from pastrami, turkey, tomatoes and Swiss cheese and handed Ben one on a plate.

'Eat up. Then go upstairs and fetch the rest of your suitcases.'

Ben didn't say anything for a moment. Then quietly he asked, 'Am I going back to school?'

'I want you to know that I've given serious consideration to your proposal of spending a "gap year" on Gemini Force One, Ben,' Truby began.

Ben felt his heart sink. Truby was gearing up to tell him that it just wasn't going to happen, that Ben had proved he couldn't be trusted.

Truby continued, 'I spoke to your Aunt Isolde. She's agreed with me that you can stay with us, if that's what you want. Kenton College have agreed, too. They'll hold a place for you for next year – if you decide to return.'

'If I decide …?' Ben felt short of breath. 'So I'm …
I'm …?'

It hardly seemed possible. He didn't dare to say the
words, in case it turned out that he'd misunderstood.

'You *are* kind of crazy, Ben! I'd have given you a
second chance, if only for Caroline's sake. But, what
you did, I have to take that into consideration, too. A
couple of oil men are home today to their wives and
kids. That's because of you. Emma has a lead on what
looks like becoming one of the biggest cases of industrial
espionage in modern times. ANPECO, well, they'll live
to fight another day, just. So – all right, kid. You're worth
a shot. It's become obvious that I need ground-pounders
as well as pilots, engineers and doctors. If we can find a
role for you, maybe we can recruit some more like you.
But you gotta work hard. And study.'

Ben nodded, his mind whirling. 'I will. You'll see.
Twenty-four seven.'

Truby seemed satisfied that they'd struck a deal. 'All
right, then. Back to GF One. You've got a busy day
tomorrow. Detailed mission debrief and analysis at eight
a.m. You should hit the gym around seven.'

Truby led him back to the Sikorsky and they took
off. Soon they were flying over the white sands and surf
of the Caribbean shore and into the night sky.

'I thought you'd be angrier,' Ben admitted, in something of a daze.

'Anger isn't useful. I burned all my anger a long time
ago. Found a way to pay it forward.'

'What happened?'

'Oh,' Truby said, softly, 'I learned a lot about all that when my brother died.'

Ben was still, suddenly aware that he was being given a rare glimpse of Truby's inner life. 'I'm sorry. How old was he?'

'We were both thirty-six. He was my twin. *Gemini*, see? We weren't identical, though, nor much alike. I was the one who got lost in engineering. Jonathan, he was the daredevil – joined the US Air Force, went to Iraq.' He paused. 'Jonathan died, shot down by Saddam's Republican Army. They think he was probably captured and tortured first. Meantime, over in Silicon Valley, I was busy making my first billion. Ain't life strange?'

'Oh, no,' breathed Ben. 'I'm really sorry.'

Across the helicopter cockpit, Truby faced him with a sad smile. 'That's war for you, Ben. Your folks didn't have much success turning you away from battle. Maybe I can give you a better alternative.'

Ben wanted to thank Truby but he was afraid that his voice might crack. Instead, he simply stared directly ahead, into the starlit sparkle of the black sea, searching for the first glimmer of the welcoming blue lights of Gemini Force One.

ACKNOWLEDGEMENTS

There was once a project with no name, Gerry Anderson's final foray into a fictional world of rescue and adventure. He'd started to think about the roots of *Thunderbirds*. How might a hi-tech global rescue agency have begun? Who would have been the first recruits? What kind of enigmatic philanthropist would have lent their name, funds and energy to rescuing people from disasters?

Disaster was to strike in Gerry's own life, in the form of Alzheimer's disease. His new story lay untouched for years: untouched but not forgotten. His son and widow, Jamie and Mary Anderson, decided that they would become custodians of Gerry's legacy. Gerry's friend, literary agent Robert Kirby, began to keep an eye open for a writer who could pick up the baton. Just before Gerry died, Robert matched me to the project.

So my first thanks are to Gerry Anderson, for caring about adventure, right to the end. I hope to do exactly the same!

To Jamie and Mary Anderson and Robert Kirby, for keeping the flame alight, for keeping the faith even when it looked as though the project we'd named 'Gemini Force One' would not find a publisher. For powering through a whirlwind Kickstarter campaign in the summer of 2013. To Emma Burch for her critical guidance and advice before and during our Kickstarter campaign. To Hannah Madsen and her team for brilliant video production, and to Gary Blackman for insisting that we go back to publishers with our Kickstarted venture.

Then, to each and every one of the Kickstarter backers, wonderful 'Anderfans' from the world over, who sent money and supportive messages, who wrote articles in newspapers, magazines, blogs. You're all part of this – thank you!

I wouldn't even have met Robert Kirby if it hadn't been for the advice and introduction from fellow children's author, Anthony Horowitz – thank you, Anthony.

Writing *Black Horizon* required me to become fairly quickly familiar with the workings of a deep-water oil platform and the mechanics of long-distance yachtsmanship. Dave Healy, an industry expert, generously talked me through the technical aspects of deep-water oil rigs. Alan Kingsman, my former biochemistry tutor at St Catherine's College, Oxford, now retired and living on a Caribbean island, shared his knowledge and experience as a solo transatlantic yachtsman to help me plot the disaster that strikes the catamaran sailors in the book.

Perhaps the most unforgettable experience of writing *Black Horizon* was the opportunity to work with legendary Hollywood designer Andrew Probert on the structure and design of the base itself, GF One. Gerry

Anderson had discussed this at length with Robert, who bequeathed these conversations to me. Andrew Probert worked to Gerry's original brief as well as the text of the novel. During transatlantic Skype conversations, Andrew introduced me to the awesome visuals of our new, fictional landscape: the setting for this and future adventures for the Gemini Force team.

Orion Publishing Group swept in like a team of superheroes, promoting GERRY ANDERSON'S GEMINI FORCE ONE to a three-book series in which we'd be able to expand all the stories for which Gerry had left fragmentary ideas. Thanks in particular to Lisa Milton and Amber Caravéo for their vision and plans for the series.

Finally, as always, I thank my husband David and daughters Josie and Lilia for their constant love and support, and patience during our summer holiday as I kept sneaking off to work on the Kickstarter campaign.

It's been a wild ride. Long may the adventures of Ben Carrington and Gemini Force One continue!

Gerry Anderson's Gemini Force One
━ The Official Kickstarter Backers List ━

This book could never have been completed without our brilliant Kickstarter backers – who believed in the project enough to put their hard-earned cash behind it to make it a reality. If you've enjoyed this book then you have all of these people to thank!

UK Conventions Limited
Jim Winch
Anonymous
Anonymous
Robert Zijderveld
Pen Turner
Nick Sofocleous
Robert Taylor
Jed Allen
Keith Hedges
Matthew Pearson
Chris Thompson
Karl Evans
Alexander Walton Kay
Sid
Geoffrey Ellis
Marty Doo
Lee Stringer
David Power
Malika Andress
Eleftherios Sarris

Rob & Spike
Graham & Katie
    Bleathman
Sylvia Paddock
Craig Greenall
Philip Rogers
Frank Collins
Nick White
Alice Prescott
Timothy Woodward
Stephen Brown
Gary Bates
Simeon Law
Felix Hemsley
Paul Stankevitch
Jim Esposito
Derek Law
Mark Dando
Ito Hidenori
Daniel Rushton
Stuart Hadley

Nigel Preece

Peter Crawford

Juan F. Herrero

Paul Gillary

Bruce Lerner

Barry G. Ford

Rebecca Fraser

Ross Webb-Wagg

Carl E. McKnight, III

Mike Wood

Joe Harwood

Adam Reed

Hal Bryan

Mark Lawrence

Chas Johnson

Keith Scott

Paul Osmond

Joe Moomin Davies

James Barclay

Derek Trapp

Thomas Benson

Mark Burton

James Willing

Steve Watts

Marc Witten

David Nightingale

Diana Webber

Tony Hardy

Ben Jones

Neil Kenny

Ian Soper

Howard Ridgwell

Laurence R. Justus

Emma Nisbet

Elliot Pavelin

Jamie Lee Vause

David Cox

Christopher Bate

Paul Simpson

Catherine Rees Lay

Gary Hodgkinson

Alex Neil

Greg Holdridge

Mark Simpson Wedge

George Hackford

Benedict Donnellan

Richard J. Bailey

Joshua & Abbie Sanders

Tim Stockford

Stephen La Riviere

Derek Harrison

Matthew Rattenbury

Christian Vitroler

Freddie Thompson

Joe McIntyre

Mark Muldowney

Austin Tate

James Longden

Simon Newton

Steve Fisher

Christopher Small

John N. Parker

Robert Jandy
Susie Day
Doug Stewart
Simon Monk
Glenn McCrabb
Dave Seymour
Jack Knoll
Douglas R. Pratt
Les Jewitt
Ray Lauff
Russell Auer
Ken L.
Steve Hochberger
George O'Hara
Jeff George
Paul Steven Dazeley
Pete Brown
Carl Green
Robin Hayes
Vic Woods
Kerrie Dougherty
Kevin Owens
David C. Pettit
Gary Dexter
Roman Andron
Alan Pike
Duncan Moss
Red Wolf
Russell Dicker
Thomas Marwede
Ryk Langton

Mark Jamie Ellie Struthers
Andrew James John
   Mackenzie
Felicity Ellis
epredator
Jamas Enright
Richard Carver
Nick Walpole
Simon Drinkwater
Ian Parry
Darren Nicholls
Geoff Dannatt
Christopher MacDonald
Ed Donnellan
Simon Belmont
Ben Hatton
Curt Holmer
Dave Fisher
Barbara Partyczna
Adrian de la Vega
Stephen Lornie
Sue & Nick Jenkins
Scott Duff
Thom Parkin
Robert Bell
Fernando Higa
Andy Starks
James Fielding
Darren Sillett
Anthony Lee
Keith Povall

John Abel
Michelle Edwards
Jeremy Chamberlain
Nicholas Foster
Sereena Burton
James Bruce
Elaine J. Jackson
Martin Nooteboom
Priscilla Lange
Phil Cragg
Graeme & Olwen Hurry
Robert Ayres
Paul J. Guest
John Brisson
Daichi Kaji
Nigel Shier
Sue Rowbotham
Chris Hart
Paul Smith
Andrew Beirne
Niek Hoeboer
Mark D. Evans
Branko Vekic
David Coddington
Jussi Myllyluoma
Martyn Grant
Mark Rescher
Jason Walker
Benjamin Diggles
Jeremy Briggs
Dr Dave Watford

Damien May
David Ahern
Ian Ayliffe
Annie Hodgson
Roger Warner
Martin Simpson
Johnathan Oldbury
Jonathan Foot
Steve Dickinson
Aidan Moran
Thomas Fitzsimons
Allan Harvey
Ken Parker
Barry John Davies
Jean Wheel
Martin Burwood
Stephen Carson
Gemma Braiding
Stephen Williams
Antony Blunt
Ross Ironfield
Patricia Caminada
Wilson Marc
Mike Dennison
Thomas Haley
Beth Howard
Karl Orbell
Lucy Jefferies
Heather Blandford
Jamie Cogan
John Freeman

Andrew Crofts
Ben Dunn
Mark Buckley
David W. Weaver
Thirzah Bragg
Brian & Maya Medlock
Hans Styrnell
Robert Lerner
Matthew Atkinson
David Broom
Derek Eaton
Bill Everatt
Art Sippo MD, MPH
Pepita Hogg-Sonnenberg
Hans de Wolf
Rob Salter
Ashley Kerrison
Nigel Critten
David Landry
Lee Cooke
Martyn Walmsley
John Nickson
Juliet Legg
Michael Zock
Douglas Smith
Jens Hildebrand
Paul Harbour
Robert Brandenburg
Antony Alldis
Andy Rolfe
Gemma Spurr

John B. Bullivant
Mark Thompson
Steve Boughton
Espen Sae-Tang
  Ottersen
Jack Norris
Chris Halliday
Chris Arnold
Andrew Clements
Lucy Jackson
Ben & Elen Roberts
Mark Joseph
Ian Jacklin
Alan C. Martin
Walter Bellini
David Gadsdon
Mike Bell
William De Micheli
Ian Cullen
Ray Horseman
Ian Coomber
Duncan Willis
Roscoe Fay
Adam McLean
Tom Forster
Andy Offor
Samuel Erskine
Don Tocher
Shane M.
Simon Wickes,
  TVCentury21.com

Teresa Freebrey
Graham M Purkiss
Wayne Simmons,
  Redmoon Interactive
Stephen Bolding
Sawako Suzuki
Mark Bailey
Omar Iqbal
Steve Berry
Dennis Burtenshaw
James Crooke
Thomas Summers
Alex Woodward
Christopher Pardy
Jay Mullins
Alexander Mullins
Stephen Billing
Aimi Brear
Nigel Heath
William Hawkins
Steve Bushell
Jason Cook
Pete Holder
James Husum
Gary Davis
Michael Grafton
Jaimi Sorrell
Emma Webster
Petrina Witt
Mark Whyte
Sean Huxter

Howard Roberts
Owen O'Sullivan
Steve Goldring
Andreas Wurzinger
Elizabeth Stanway
Ian Greig
Lin Dowse
Joe La Touche
Clyde Soesan
Miles J. Moody
Richard Tomsett
Donna-Marie Lawrence
Michael Bates
Sam Ledwich
Derek Mayne
Ian Martin
John Roney
Alexander Worton
Richard Petts
Ian McCabe
David Smith
Alison Muir &
  Deborah Topp
Robert Wood
Cameron Paine
Daren Dochterman
Aaron Cattermer
Dave Girling
Jonathan Baxter
John Reed
Derek Traynor

Chris Bishop
Kevin Mayle
Amy Holland
Nick Havard
Tobias Bergström
Langtec Limited
Andrew Staton
Allan Bott
Stuart Mitchell
Stephen A. Hollingdale
Mike Jones
Rayna Harris
Paul Welsby
Kees Koenen
Magdalena Plebans
Garry Vaux
Gordon Aitken
Neil Jackson
Anthony Flynn
Charles C. Albritton, III
Joseph Marsden
Raymond Micallef
Elliott Webb
Josiah Knight
Colin Bayliss
Robert Vasey
C. Beckford
Merv Staton
Roy Beaufoy
Michael Paschetag
Chris Potter

Sam Armitage
Elliot Lewis Wainwright
Andy Hamilton
Ian Parmenter
Neil Calton
Alex Webster
Adrian Bird
Richard Fannon
Lucas Bendict Francis
Nino Spellman Welsh
Charles Barnard
David Leech
Timon Proctor
Stuart Hannah
Christian Tarpey
Phil Stevens
David Wright
Marcus Gipps
Maurice Young
Tim Pollard
Konstantin Gorelyy
Will Morris
Jason Sperber
Blair Winton
Nye Marks
Andrew Kenny
Dave Healy
Mark Rowe
Paul Dent
Peter L. Brown
Richard T. Yelland

Dennis J. Sycamore
Mike Davey
Peter Noble
Keith Gooch
Wellesley Watkins
Julian Benton
Mike Ellis
Chris Beckett
Helen Watt
Joseph Coen
Emily & Brinly Meldon
Mark Davys
J.G.L. Colle
Chris Zaremba
Gary W. Bacon
Pierre Pascal
Chris Gerard
Helen Collins
Matt Grandis
Jean-Pierre Bacash
Thomas Coates
Rupert Fuller
Craig Schloman
Robert Hill
Dominic Riley
Paul H. Colbeck
Einar Petersen
John N. Perrin

Damien 'DarkenedD'
   Cheetham
Malcolm Watson
Sean Jones
T. Taylor
Mark Farrell
David Folgate
Lars Fikenscher
David Dmytriw
John G. Wilkinson
David Schutt
Eileen Skidmore
Giovanni Lani
Christopher Sykes
Nigel Fairhurst
Mark Kilfoil
Robert Kirby
Connie Dunne
Martin V. Young
David Moffatt
Mamas Pitsillis
Paul Holder
Mike Kirkham-Ingram
Ian Stopher
Gary Sullivan
Richard Thorpe
Stuart Drummond
Orlando Brown

the orion star

★ ★ ★

CALLING ALL GROWN-UPS!
Sign up for **the orion star** newsletter to
hear about your favourite authors and exclusive
competitions, plus details of how children
can join our 'Story Stars' review panel.

Sign up at:

www.orionbooks.co.uk/orionstar

Follow us 🐦 @the_orionstar
Find us 📘 facebook.com/TheOrionStar